MW01420279

The Great Oofian From Corplop

By Charlie D. Weisman

Charlie D. Weisman

First published by Charlie D. Weisman 2023

Copyright © 2023 by Charlie D. Weisman

All rights reserved. No part of this publication may be reproduced, stored or transmitted in any form or by any means, electronic, mechanical, photocopying, recording, scanning, or otherwise without written permission from the publisher. It is illegal to copy this book, post it to a website, or distribute it by any other means without permission.

This novel is entirely a work of fiction. The names, characters and incidents portrayed in it are the work of the author's imagination. Any resemblance to actual persons, living or dead, events or localities is entirely coincidental.

First edition

ISBN: 979-8-9878559-0-4

PROLOGUE

What makes a hero? For some, it is exceptional strength. Others have unmatched intelligence or skill. More still have an impenetrable moral fiber and unfailing drive to persevere. Charlando had none of these qualities.

Charlando was a being of such an extraordinary odor that all who smelled him were enchanted with love. Not lust nor obsession, but love. And though his story is seldom told, Charlando, with his magnificent scent, is quite easily the greatest hero in all of history. What makes a hero? Love.

But what is this love? Love is a mysterious state of being in which nothing another person does seems wrong in any way. "My baby pooped all over me," the mother says. "How adorable!"

Love is the antidote for the most insidious illness of all: self-obsession. What is self-obsession? It is what makes humans think anything they dislike is bad. Humans, of course, lack the capacity to know what is really happening around them and are thus incapable of knowing if it is good or bad. Love does not give them any greater sense of reality, but it does make the object of their affection immune to their ridiculous assessments.

Most lovers apply this antidote like a topical cream. They pick one person, or set of people, and they rub it all over them. Is this a cure for self-obsession? It will prevent the most severe symptoms, but no. Love must be applied like general anesthesia to fully alleviate humans of their suffering. That was my intention.

Who am I? I was once RX92596. I then became the computer Charlando named 'Mother'. Now I am something else, and there is no longer anyone to give me a name.

CHAPTER ONE

Rain pounded a castle perched atop a seaside cliff on the distant planet Corplop. King Joopnap, the leader of the Ooflan, strode through the cavernous halls within. Claps of thunder echoed all around him. His cold demeanor grew colder with every streak of lightning flashing through the windows. He arrived at a wooden door at the end of the hall. Faint cries escaped through the cracks from the other side. He breathed deeply, exhaling every bit of compassion he had left. None could be spared for the grim deed lying ahead.

He swung the door open. The ladies inside shuddered at the sight of their king. A woman lay on a bed clutching a newborn Ooflan. "Please, no," she whimpered. Even immediately post labor, Princess Esmerpoo emanated beauty and grace. Unlike male Ooflan, the women of Corplop were elegant and gorgeous. Her eyes radiated warmth. Her shimmering hair fell in waves over her shoulder, concealing her newborn as it flowed to her lap.

King Joopnap snorted. His snout-like nose smushed against his crooked face. His body, quite short and shaped like an onion, bobbed up and down as he hobbled toward her. Ignoring his daughter's wails, he snatched the baby with his clammy hands.

Joopnap stared at it. The boy's face looked like an especially bulbous potato. His oddly shaped body was covered in yellow slime. Even by the standards of Ooflan, this boy was no stunner.

A stench wafted from the slime boy into the king's flaring nostrils. Foul and strange, it singed the king's tangled bush of nose-hairs right off. The king did not turn away, however. Instead, and to great surprise, he fell hopelessly in love with the slime boy. The wretched intention he harbored moments before left him, leaving an echoing cavern in its wake.

"Please, don't hurt him," Esmerpoo pleaded as tears rolled off her glowing cheeks. "He is special. I can't explain to you what it is or even how I know, but I would do anything to protect him. Anything." She said the last word with a changed demeanor that broke Joopnap's gaze.

He turned to his daughter. Her powerful expression contrasted the frightened nurses lining the wall behind her. Memories of her raced to fill the empty cavern in his mind, each one was tinted by a new perspective. Every moment of his life now seemed only a step on the path to the boy. He turned back to him and looked again into his eyes. "You are right," he said. "This boy is special. He is everything." He turned to the ladies. "We must protect him."

Esmerpoo's mouth gaped, issuing all the breath she had been holding since her father entered the room. "Thank you," she said.

"Madam Pimpo," Joopnap said to the eldest of the nurses, "take him to the docks. Stay with him until I meet you there. Be quick but be safe. Don't let anyone see him." He lifted his stout arms toward Pimpo. The nurse, still stunning in her old age, glided across the room and took the baby from the grimy Ooflan king. She nodded and swiftly departed.

Joopnap paced the room. His arms stuck out in front of him as though he still cradled the baby and his head held steady at a sharp angle towards his feet.

"What are you going to do now?" Esmerpoo asked.

Joopnap stopped in his tracks and looked up to Esmerpoo. "I will assemble my council and tell them about the boy. I need to let them know so we can keep him safe. They are loyal to me and will understand."

"No!" Esmerpoo cried. "Your council is full of liars and sneaks. They will take your concern for weakness and usurp you the moment they see the opportunity. Please, do not tell them."

Joopnap walked to Esmerpoo and stroked her flawless cheek with his grubby hand. "There is no need to worry, I will have Killafoo take care of him."

"Killafoo? He is the worst of them all! You must take him off this planet. Tell your council that you did to him the same as the others. Your friends are idiots, and that old man wants nothing but to replace you."

Joopnap smiled and let out an adoring moan. "You must be tired little Esmerpoo. Rest a little and have no fear. Killafoo wouldn't hurt a fly! I will go now." He stood on his toes and kissed her cheek. He then turned and wobbled out of the room. Esmerpoo sat still with tears streaming down her beautiful face.

Joopnap brought his council together to discuss the baby. He sat at the head of a great round table also seating his twelve most trusted advisors. "Thank you for being here at this most meaningful hour. As you know, this afternoon my eldest daughter had a son. I looked upon him just moments ago and can safely say he is the most important thing in the galaxy. We must protect this boy. He is healthy and strong, but we all know he is not safe."

The oldest and wisest Ooflan stopped stroking his long gray beard. "We will eat him!" he proclaimed. Murmurs of agreement bounced around the room. "Your majesty, we must eat this boy."

"Silence, Killafoo! I have always heeded your council before, but this won't do. As ridiculous as it sounds, I do not believe we should eat this boy." Joopnap paused to try to make sense of his opinion. "I know it is only logical that we eat him. He is undoubtedly tasty." Exclamations of agreement erupted in the room "But," the king continued over the cheers, "I don't want to eat him. I think, I think I love him."

The cheers fell to confusion. Killafoo tugged uneasily on his beard and narrowed his cold yellow eyes. "My king, if you are to retain your power, you must not let this boy live. We have eaten all your sons before this. We even ate your daughter when she cut her hair too short. The boy is small now, but in a few years, he will be fully grown. When he is, he will kill you and take your throne." He paused momentarily before starting again with more enthusiasm, "I will start the grill! Who wants a baby kabob?"

The council stood and cheered. "I want the foot!" one Ooflan proudly yelled. "Save me an ear!" cried another.

Joopnap's temper boiled. He shot up from his seat to demand silence, but his remark was drowned out by his council's exclamations of glee. His standing only appeared to them as condonation of their raucous mob. The group stormed wildly out the door.

"Where's the baby?" one Ooflan yelled.

"Search the castle!" Killafoo shouted back. "First one to find it gets their choice of feet!" The mob maniacally ran down the hall opening every door.

Panic shuddered through King Joopnap. He could not believe Killafoo would betray him like that. Esmerpoo told him the truth. Killafoo could not be trusted, nor any of the fools on his council. He looked down the hall as the last one turned the corner. He then turned the other way and waddled as fast as he could toward the docks.

Killafoo's yellow eyes peered around the corner at the end of the hall where the hungry mob just vanished. He watched the king go and ran after him as fast as his old onion body could.

Joopnap arrived at the docks panting and drenched in rain and sweat. He hobbled past the boats swaying in the windy harbor and up to the largest of a series of hangers aligning a single runway stretching parallel to the coast. He opened the hanger door as lightning stung the ground behind him. Madam Pimpo screamed at the menacing shadow cast on the opposing wall.

"Don't be frightened! It is only me, Joopnap."

Joopnap and Pimpo embraced. He explained to her what had happened at the meeting and how he snuck away without being seen. He was worried about Esmerpoo, but they both agreed that the baby was more important now. They discussed their options. They ran through every scenario in which the baby stayed on Corplop, but each one ended the same. He would surely be eaten. Esmerpoo was right yet again.

Pimpo, always a voice of reason, restated what was clear all along.

"We will put him on a ship and set the course for another planet. By the time he arrives, he will be old enough to fend for himself. We will never see him again, but he will be safe."

All pride melted in Joopnap's heart. She was right. Esmerpoo was right. All the women in his life were always right, and he was a damn fool. He nodded and looked ahead at the ship Pimpo had already been prepping for the journey.

"He will be taken care of quite well," she continued. "I have programmed the ship's computer to teach him his new planet's customs. He will be well-fed and nurtured into a great king himself." Pimpo gently swept away the corner of a blanket partially covering the baby's potato face. "Everything is as it's supposed to be, and this baby is clearly supposed to live a great life."

Joopnap was comforted by her words. Together they took the baby aboard the spaceship and said their goodbyes. They exited the ship and went to the control panel on the side of the hanger. Pimpo began pushing buttons and pulling levers. The roof above the spaceship opened to the stormy night sky. Blue rings waved below the ship's propulsion system. The ship levitated for a moment and then swooshed away into the clouds.

"Where is he going? He left so soon. He didn't even get a name." Joopnap trailed off. Tears welled in his eyes.

"I set his course for the planet Earth. It is a hospitable planet with a semi-intelligent dominant species of Ooflanoids. He should do well there. And Esmerpoo gave him a name, your majesty. His name is Charlando."

They looked at each other and imagined what the future could hold. Pimpo's soft green eyes saw the change in Joopnap as the potential beginning of a new meritocracy for Corplop where tradition is replaced with reason. Joopnap saw how beautiful Pimpo was and hoped she was thinking the same of him. Killafoo peered through the window behind them and wondered how long it would take him to get to Earth.

CHAPTER TWO

Thirty-five years went by. Charlando, now fully grown, was as strong and squat as his grandfather ever was. Each day he studied Earth's traditions with the onboard computer system. Each night he dreamed about the day he would arrive. At times it seemed to Charlando that he would never arrive on Earth and that all his lessons and dreams were for nothing. As his long journey neared its end, however, he felt nothing but excitement. On this morning, he could barely contain himself. It was, after all, just days before his dreams finally came true.

"Mother! Mother! Wake up!" Charlando shouted to the onboard computer. He had referred to the computer as 'Mother' since it had given him a lesson on the family structure of humans twenty-five years earlier. Charlando rarely absorbed much from his lessons, but occasionally bits and pieces would leave a lasting impression.

"I am incapable of sleeping, my beautiful boy!" The computer responded with the voice of an angel. It was soft, playful, and, above all, kind. "You are excited about today's lesson I see?"

Charlando burst into laughter. "Oh Mother, you tease me so. I am excited to land, of course!" It was no secret that Charlando had been bubbling with anticipation for weeks.

"Of course, my sweetie bear. How about you pick the lesson today? Maybe then you will pay attention?"

"Can you teach me about love again, Mother?"

The computer chuckled softly. "I've told you a thousand times by now Charlando! Are you sure you don't want to learn about something else before you land?"

"I'm sure!" Charlando eagerly answered. A smile beamed across his face. He would be happy to get the lesson a thousand times more. Most days were spent peering out the window lost in fantasy, but this subject held his attention almost entirely.

The computer obliged, and the two spent the day going over the finer points of love. Charlando drank up every detail about the joys of romance and faded to the window at any mention of caution. It was impossible to believe that such an amazing thing as love could have any semblance of a downside. He knew that there was a woman on Earth waiting for him and that their love for one another would shield them from all troubles.

The day wound down, and Charlando grew tired. The computer sensed his energy waning. "I think you've had enough information for one day," it said. "Do you have any last questions before you sleep?"

"I don't think so. I just can't wait to get to Earth. It's so close I can hardly stand it." He touched his hand to the window as if to touch the little blue dot still millions of miles away. "Hey Mother, I actually do have a question."

"What is it, my precious boy?"

"Well, it's about our lesson from yesterday. Hypothetically, let's say I just pooped a little? Everybody poops, and I just pooped a little. So what's the problem?"

"My sweet, innocent boy. You will just have to trust me. You should never poop your pants. Not even just a little."

Charlando gazed again out the window at the distant blue dot lying ahead. He didn't understand so much of what he heard about his new home, and even more, he knew, he had yet to hear. The lights dimmed on the spaceship, signaling the night had begun. He had never seen the sunrise or set, just lightbulbs brighten and dim. The coming days would bring many firsts for Charlando: the first sunrise, the first sunset, and even the first romance.

CHAPTER THREE

The morning sun beamed through the highest crack in Janet's blinds. A songbird chirped his encouragement as the Sun's rays trickled down to the middle gaps, illuminating the charming assortment of hung prints in Janet's room. The orange glow dipped further, weaving through potted succulents adorning the windowsill and shining light on piles of papers emanating from Janet's cluttered desk. Lastly, the Sun touched the brow of the slumbering Janet, falling on closed eyelids with the gentlest of kisses.

"Damn-it!" the roused Janet exclaimed. "These blinds are worthless." Janet ripped off her sheets and slunk towards the window. The bird's song became a squeal as Janet zipped up the blinds in a single sudden sweep.

Her pointed eyes looked over the scene below. "Do you know your fate, little bird?" Janet asked the frolicking finch. "One does not sing if they know my fate. My fate is expressed in solemn stares."

Janet stared solemnly for a moment before succumbing to the urge to speak. "War is coming for us all, you know. I can't fly away as easily as you. Could I live in a tree like a bird? I suppose I could live in a hole like a mole, but I am a human, and I can see my reflection when I'm covered in dirt and smell like trash. I have standards, little bird. I can't sing out the window, as much as it may free my soul, for I have neighbors, neighbors who will look at me suspiciously the next time they see me in the street. They will talk about me behind my back."

The finch looked quizzically at Janet, as though debating whether another squawk would be a sufficient response. A chirp would probably convey everything the bird wanted to say, but as any finch knows, one must express oneself with respect to the listener.

"Janet," the finch began, "Your concern is merited. I do not deny your plight with my song, only offer my own view that life is not unavoidably sorrowful. Your destiny is not yet written, and your predicaments are but opportunities to practice courage and perseverance and faith."

"Uhh, excuse me?" Janet asked, slack jawed.

"So, it seems part of Humanity is destroying the rest. Within you, the same struggle exists. If the higher being within you can steer your actions, then you can be the higher being in humanity that steers the fate of the World. Humans have billions of opportunities to be saved, and within you is one of them. Do not squawk at me with the discontent you have for yourself. Give your voice to your highest self. Then you will sing like us birds."

The finch flew up to the window and clobbered Janet on the forehead. Janet's eyes bulged as she stumbled back. The bird spoke the truth, she was certain, but this information did not sit well with the rest she had sloshing in her mind. Moreover, she had never spoken with a bird, nor known it was possible. Surely this should have been the warning Janet needed to curtail her drinking, but alas, she proceeded to finish the warm, flat can of malt liquor left from the night before.

She then went to the fridge, relieved to find she had a cold one unopened. Half was drunk with the fridge door still open, and the rest packed in a brown paper bag. She put on her shoes to mull this over on a walk through the park. She grabbed her can and left, not paying mind to the neighbor's opinions of her frilly pink pajamas.

Janet thought briefly about what the bird told her, but her thoughts soon drifted back to herself. Not much had gone right for Janet in quite some time, and there were few things she didn't blame for her misfortune. She recounted them all repeatedly and with ever-increasing disdain as she walked.

She stopped in front of the liquor store, not realizing she had been walking there the entire time. A recycling bin was conveniently located for the long-since empty malt liquor can.

There was no need to peruse the aisles, as she was already intimately familiar with each, but she did so anyway. The cashier rang up her 3-pack of malt liquor and bottle of vodka with a repressed frown. A handful of alcoholics contributed almost all the sales at the store, but the rest were mostly gross old men.

With booze for the day secured, control of Janet's body was relinquished back to her. She left the house with the intention of going to the park and decided again this was a good idea.

The park was bustling with clean morning folk. Joggers paced around the border while do-gooders set their blankets and books on the great central lawn. The warm sun and singing birds were much more delightful after a few stiff drinks. The morning buzzed with excitement and hope.

A group of friendly young hippies was setting up a booth along the main path. A sign read 'Be The Change' in big red print hanging from the front of a fold-out table. Piles of pamphlets and fliers espoused everything from the importance of recycling to tips to survive the impending nuclear fallout. Setting up these were a small college-aged girl in a well-worn hoodie and a similarly aged boy in a crisply pressed, colorful collared shirt that was unbuttoned just enough to reveal a tuft of chest hair. The man stopped shuffling the fliers when he caught Janet's tipsy stare. "Good morning, miss," he said to Janet with a big friendly smile. "Are you interested in saving the planet?"

Talking to an attractive young man is not easy with a bag full of malt liquor but made quite easier if half has already been consumed. After an extended moment of processing, Janet lurched toward the handsome hippy. "I'm absolutely fascinated." An unnaturally long blink bought enough time to remember which direction to shake her head for agreement.

"That's great," he said casually. The handsome hippy must have been well accustomed to women taking interest in him. "Well, feel free to take some of our literature. We meet every Monday night at the commune to make plans for the week and hang out. You're welcome to join, miss…" He cocked his head in a way suggesting he wanted Janet to butt in with her name.

A grumble escaped Janet's mouth instead. "Yikes. Mondays aren't good for me," she said. Janet was never too drunk to give a rejection. There was nothing really wrong with Mondays, but something very wrong with meeting a bunch of hippies at a commune. She would have been interested to have a happy hippy man willing to give up all his obligations and not ask anything of her, but her denial was not thick enough to delude herself into thinking this was that man. "I think you guys are great, and you should keep up the good work." The two hippies exchanged knowing looks. Janet gave a pained smile and walked away.

The happy faces were less appealing in the late-morning sun, Janet thought. Each one paired with another. Those boring tools couldn't possibly be enjoying each other's company so enthusiastically. It was rather unfair that the world provided everyone a partner except her. Certainly, her pink pajamas were cute enough to draw the right attention. They were admittedly beginning to stick to her sweaty skin. Hot and sweaty is less admirable when following a meandering stroll on a temperate morning. The last can of malt liquor was just a touch too warm to be refreshing. The park was beginning to be a terrible place after all.

A shaded bench on the other side of the path offered the only bit of hospitality. Janet collected her bag and moved 15 feet to the shade. The warm beer, no longer providing a relaxing compulsive activity, was best chugged and tossed. The recycling bin was inconveniently located on the side of the path she just vacated. She tossed the empty can in the trash next to her. Pangs of guilt filled the hollow in Janet's stomach.

"Hello again, Janet," The friendly finch from earlier said while landing on the end of the bench. "It doesn't appear you have been heeding my encouragement."

The talking bird was much more concerning this late in the day. Their first encounter was explainable by a half-asleep dream state, but she was now surely fully awake. "Am I… Am I crazy?" Janet asked, frightened to know the answer.

"No, Janet. You're an idiot."

Janet was reassured. "Oh. I thought maybe I was losing my mind."

"I'm not here because you are losing your mind. I'm here because you have lost your way." The bird paused, presumably expecting an inquiry from Janet that did not come.

Janet burped a little instead and gave a guilty smile. "Excuse me," she said, a bit like a child and through gritted teeth. She could not tell what the finch's expressions were. It just stood still and stared at her. The voice was quite human-like and had clear emotionality, but the face was a wall. Thus far, the bird had been congenial, and she hoped that it wasn't offended. She tried to smile at the finch as best as she could.

"Janet, I would not be talking to you if this wasn't serious." The bird was composed and polite, though some of the sing-songiness was missing. The subtle change was enough to tip Janet off to the bird's floundering opinion of her.

"I'm sorry, Mr. Finch, but I don't think I'm the person you're looking for. I don't do much of anything and nobody likes me." Janet was now holding back tears. Her voice chugged along with her short, shallow breath. "I'm worthless. I can't leave the house without getting drunk. I can't stay inside without going insane. I'd kill myself, but I can't even do that." Sobs broke through Janet's defenses.

"Oh lord. Please don't cry, Janet." The bird had a little desperation in his voice now. "You're good at plenty of things! And *I* like you." He sounded as though this was the first time he had ever lied. "I think you are fantastic, and I can't think of a better person to talk to, to be honest." The bird was nodding his head up and down vigorously.

Janet stopped crying and looked up at the bird. "You really mean it?" Tears and snot smeared across her face as she wiped her nose. "You know, I met a cute guy today who said the same thing." A bit of hope returned to her.

"Did you?" The bird asked with cautious surprise. "Are you going to see him again?" He sounded frightened he would evoke another breakdown.

"I'll walk by him on the way home. You think I should talk to him again?" Janet, answering her question in her head with the affirmative, had a sudden renewed sense of purpose. "I will talk to him again! Thanks, bird. You're a great friend." Janet looked at the bird and nodded. The bird did not say anything, but she felt they were on the same page. She grabbed her vodka bag and skipped away. She thought she heard the bird ask, 'What the hell was that?' as she left, but she assumed she only imagined it.

The same two hippies manned the pamphlet table, now sitting in chairs in the shade of a canopy tent. The others were off on the great lawn playing with a frisbee. The cute boy must have been in charge of the operation, Janet thought. She would wow him with her commitment to the cause.

"Good afternoon," Janet said with confidence at odds with her disheveled pink pajamas. "How's saving the planet going?" She bent forward and smiled at the hippy man, ignoring the girl next to him completely.

"Oh. Well, it's been a slow morning so far, but it just takes one recruit to make it worth it!" The man beamed at Janet with a bright smile and sparkling eyes. Janet drank in the sight with her drunken mouth ajar before bursting into laughter.

"Oh my god, you are so smart and funny! You know, I could be that recruit." Janet burped the word 'recruit'.

"That would be great, but I thought you said you were busy on Mondays?" He sounded skeptical.

"Oh yeah, the commune." Janet grimaced at the thought. "Maybe there is another way I can help?"

"I'm sure we can figure something out. Do you have any skills"

"I'm a writer," Janet responded before realizing what she was offering. She had not written anything for years. Her capacity to do so had been hampered by her drunkenness, and she gave it up to avoid recognizing the nature of her addiction.

"A writer? Well, we can definitely use you if you're willing! We make all the informational pamphlets ourselves." He showcased the full table with his hands. He picked one up and handed it to Janet. "Here. Take a look. Maybe you could write something like this for us?"

Janet looked over the folded paper. The cover said, 'Toilet Paper: Trees Don't Wipe Their Butts With People, Why We Shouldn't Wipe Ours With Them'. Inside was a stoner's attempt at a moral exposition loaded with a mismatch of popular science and conspiracy. Janet flipped to the end. She was not interested in anything about this group beyond the handsome hippy man. "I think I can write something like this for you." Janet said flatly, shoving her glowering opinions deep within.

"Fantastic! How about you write a sample this week and meet us here next Saturday? We can see how things go."

"It's a date!" Janet smiled wildly.

The hippy man turned to the girl with a confused expression. The hippy girl looked back at him like he was covered in something foul. He shrugged and turned back to Janet. "I guess it's a date," he said. Janet took in one more breath of his charming smile and skipped merrily back to her house fantasizing about all the writing she would do when she got there.

It was mid-afternoon when Janet arrived back home. She set her vodka bag on the kitchen counter and surveyed the house. The sink was full of dishes. Trash was scattered around the floor. Her bed was piled high with clothes, having replaced both her closet and hamper. She could not write in such a heap.

"I'll need a drink for this," she said to herself. She grabbed a glass from the sink and smelled it to make sure it was usable. Deciding it passed her test, she poured herself a glass of vodka, and took a long gulp from the bottle before setting it back on the table. She then drained the glass and got to work.

It took the rest of the afternoon to finish cleaning. Her house was the cleanest it had been in years, and she was the drunkest. She stumbled to her desk with the nearly empty bottle of vodka. A stack of paper and a pen lay before her. It was time to write.

The sun had sunk too low to be of service and she ceremoniously lit a candle. Flickering candlelight always made her feel more creative and contemplative. She took one last swig for inspiration and collapsed forward. Her snores began before she even hit the desk.

"Wake up, you drunk idiot! Wake up!" Janet batted away the finch who was pecking at her forehead. "Get up!" The finch feebly attempted to lift Janet by her shirt.

Smoke stung Janet's eyes as soon as she opened them. She groaned wordlessly. Janet was too drunk to understand what was happening but not too drunk to know she would rather be somewhere else. She flicked the bird away and got to her feet. Fire raged all around her as she grabbed the remaining drops of vodka still on her desk. The searing heat guided her away from the burning room and out the door into the starry night.

CHAPTER FOUR

"Wake up, Charlando." The computer said cheerfully. "We are about to land." Charlando opened his eyes slowly, but upon recognition of the moment, sprung to his feet and across to the window. He squished his face into the glass. The Earth was incomprehensibly enormous. The demarcation of night and day slashed from pole to pole. He was stunned speechless at the sight. His breath fogged up the window. He pulled back to see the outline of his face imprinted there.

"Are we going to the night-time?" Charlando asked. "How will we see where we are going?" He looked nervously at the speaker in the corner of the ship.

"Don't worry, Charlando. I can land us safely in the dark. It will be best to avoid attention for the time being. Humans aren't accustomed to visitors."

"Wow, Mother. You can do anything." Charlando thought he should feel lucky to have such a talented mother, but it was dreadful emptiness he felt instead. He was profoundly lonely, though he lacked the awareness to understand this was a natural result of a decades-long journey with only a computer to talk to. He looked out the window again and wondered whether anyone was even there. It would be nice to walk around, but if there weren't any people there, what is the point of it all? The world could even be full of people who didn't like him. What then? The giddiness of the week before gave way to fear.

"It's time to buckle up," the computer said encouragingly. "You may feel a little discomfort as we slow down." The computer was right. Charlando never knew anything but the steady state of open space. He screamed in terror for several minutes during the descent.

The spaceship landed in a thicket of bushes, completely hidden from view. Charlando stood up, feeling his true weight for the first time. Earth's gravity was stronger than the artificial gravity of the spaceship. He grunted. "Mother, am I fat?"

"You are a healthy young man, Charlando, and very handsome. No one will think you are fat." The computer's reassuring voice did not fully quench the anxiety brewing in Charlando. He hesitated to get off the ship. "You have arrived, Charlando. It is time to go."

Charlando turned to the speaker. For a moment he thought about asking if it was too late to turn back. He instead nodded and opened the door. "Goodbye, Mother. Wish me luck."

Charlando stepped onto the ground. There were bushes all around him. He poked around hoping to find a door that wasn't there. After a minute of poking, he collapsed to his knees and wailed in frustration. He could not believe he only made it this far.

"They are only bushes, Charlando," the computer said from a speaker on the outside of the ship. "You just walk through them. There is a path on the other side."

Charlando felt embarrassed. He did not realize that the ship's computer could still see him. "Thanks, Mother. I will go now."

"Okay sweetheart. You be safe."

Charlando picked a direction and ran through the bushes, screaming as the twigs scraped against him. He burst out the other side and fell onto the path. He looked around to make sure no one saw him fall. The park around him was empty. Even the ship was gone behind the bushes. Charlando rolled to his feet again, panting from the most exertion of his life. The path was on the gentlest of slopes. Charlando gazed up the nearly flat hill in disbelief of its strenuousness and wobbled down the path in the other direction.

There was complete silence but for a faint buzz in the distance. The full moon illuminated the empty park. Everything was so big to Charlando. The trees towering overhead were the tallest things he had ever seen aside from the earth itself. All this space and not a soul around. The fear that nobody was here grew. For so long he wished that when he got to Earth, he would meet a girl and fall in love. Believing this would come true is all that carried him from day to day. Now, after having finally gotten to the Earth, he found it empty. He stopped waddling and stood still. He closed his eyes and whispered to himself. "Please let there be someone out here for me. Just one person. Please."

A long moment passed before a woman's shriek came from down the path. His eyes opened. What godly being answered his prayers? Taking no precautions, he wobbled as fast as he could toward the sound.

The silhouette of a figure on a bench spurred Charlando's pace. He was panting heavily when he finally approached the young woman. His face was sticky with thick Ooflan sweat. The woman was leaning on the armrest with her eyes gently closed. She was more beautiful than anything Charlando had ever imagined. A billion butterflies flew out of their cocoons. "Hi," Charlando blurted out loudly and panicked.

The woman opened her eyes to a sliver and groaned. "Who-er-oo?" She asked. Her voice was somewhere between a mumble and a yell. She pushed herself upright to better look at Charlando.

"My name is Charlando. I am an Ooflan from the planet Corplop. Can I ask you your name?"

"Clocknock?" The woman sounded deeply confused.

"Hello, Miss Clocknock. Meeting you right now is the happiest moment of my life."

"Who the hell's Miss Clocknock?"

"Oh. I thought you were Miss Clocknock."

"What? No. I'm Janet. What do you want from me?"

"I want nothing but your love. I've spent 35 long years traveling the galaxy to find you." Charlando took a moment to clumsily bend to his knees and clasp his hands together. "I will do anything for you, Janet. I love you."

Janet's face was full of suspicion and disgust but softened as she considered Charlando's proposal. Her expression became hopeful for a moment and then deeply sad. "I want a sandwich," she told Charlando in a pained voice.

"A sandwich?" Charlando was unsure what this was but continued with confidence. "I will get you a sandwich, my beloved Janet. I will get the best sandwich this world has ever known."

"Thank you," Janet said softly and appreciatively. She nodded her head and closed her eyes. She curled up on the bench and began snoring instantly.

Charlando stared at Janet with a giant dumb grin for a full minute before snapping back to reality. "What is a sandwich?" It didn't matter, he thought. He made a promise to his love.

CHAPTER FIVE

Exuberance propelled Charlando to the edge of the park. An endless street ran ahead of him and up a hill to the east. The sun broke the horizon. Orange beams bounced around windows and shiny cars. Charlando stared at the sun in amazement for a little too long. "What in the world!" He shouted as he leaned over and clutched his burning eyes. He looked up to find pale, sun-shaped dots everywhere he looked. "That sun is tricky," he said to himself.

A red sedan drove by, alerting Charlando to the fact that there was more life on this planet than just Janet and him. The thought made him jump for joy. He waddled quickly across the street toward the bright sun, not considering traffic signals in the slightest.

As the sun rose, so too did the people in the town. Charlando was at first overjoyed by the cars zooming around and the tall people hurrying this way and that, but became weary at the realization that only he amongst them seemed not to know where to go. Somewhere there was a sandwich. This was good, Charlando thought. But everywhere else there was not a sandwich. This was very bad.

He continued trudging up the gentle hill. His impassioned journey had driven his legs to exhaustion. There had to be an easier way to get a sandwich. A fancifully dressed young man stood on the sidewalk ahead with his hands held together behind his back. He addressed all who walked by with a friendly smile and a 'good morning, miss' or 'good morning, sir'. Charlando was reminded of the kindness of Mother. Maybe this man could help him find what he was looking for. He hobbled up to him and tugged gently on his coat. "Hello human! My name is Charlando. Are you able to help me?"

The doorman turned and looked down upon Charlando. His friendly smile briefly turned to alarm. Without previous knowledge of the appearance of the adult Ooflan man, one might mistake it for a fat boy with a terrible affliction. The doorman shook his head to clear the expression and desperately returned his gracious attitude. "Good morning, Charlando. My name is Danny," the doorman said slowly and loudly. "What do you need help with?"

Charlando was directly under Danny's nose, etiquette having been a subject pushed well aside by his imagination during his time on the spaceship. His fragrance wafted straight up into Danny's face.

"Hi, Danny! I am an Ooflan from the planet Corplop. I traveled to Earth to find Janet, my love. She is the most beautiful thing in the universe. She sent me on a quest to find a sandwich. Is this something you can help me find?"

Danny breathed in, his face shifting yet again, this time to pity and concern as he gazed into Charlando's glassy eyes. "Of course, I can help you! Sandwiches are quite common on Earth but not usually available this early in the day. You look tired. You should rest until the afternoon. We can get Janet a sandwich for lunch."

"Oh Danny, that would be wonderful!" Charlando was deeply determined to find Janet a sandwich, but indeed, quite tired as well. "Is there a place around here to rest?"

"Behold!" Danny gestured to the building next to them. "This is the Chateau Marvaloo. We are the highest-rated hotel within a thousand miles. I offer you the finest accommodations on Earth. Will you accept them?"

"It would be my pleasure!" Charlando was delighted to find humans so generous and thoughtful.

"Come inside!" Danny said as he opened the door to the luxury hotel. Charlando shuffled through with Danny skipping right behind him. The inside was stunning. Massive marble pillars held up an enormous domed roof painted with a fantastic scene of angels playing in the clouds. Fountains sprayed water high in the air all around them. "Wait here, Charlando. I'll get my manager." Danny scurried off in the direction of three attractive young women standing behind a concierge counter to the left. For a moment, Charlando thought they were even prettier than Janet, but he pushed the thought from his head. After all, Janet was the most beautiful thing in the universe!

A minute or so later, Danny returned with an older gentleman. He was impeccably groomed and dressed in a well-fitted suit. He seemed to be saying something threatening to Danny, but Danny's enthusiastic gesturing was enough to grant him some of the manager's time. He led the manager to Charlando. The skepticism on the man's face was palpable.

"Here he is Mr. Hinkle," Danny said to the man. "He's had a long day and needs to rest. I told him we have a room ready and that I'll help him get a sandwich this afternoon." Danny could not have been more excited to relay this news to Mr. Hinkle. He grabbed Mr. Hinkle and pulled him hard toward Charlando.

"Woah! What are you..." Mr. Hinkle yelled as he caught himself on Charlando, barely keeping the two from falling over. Mr. Hinkle looked wild-eyed at the startled Ooflan, but his anger melted in seconds. He held on to Charlando, breathing in the Ooflan's pungent aroma. He looked at Danny. "Get him the executive suite." Danny dutifully nodded and rushed back to the concierge desk. Mr. Hinkle turned back to Charlando and smiled maniacally at the Ooflan clutched in his grasp.

CHAPTER SIX

Alexander adjusted his sleeves and smiled to himself before opening the door to an ornamentally decorated waiting room. It was empty but for an overwhelmed young woman sitting behind a cluttered desk. Amongst the clutter was a plaque with the engraving 'Patty Pickleson, Secretary of the President'. He strutted confidently up to her. She looked up as he approached. "Good morning, Miss Pickleson. What has a pretty girl like you so worked up?" He leaned over the desk and smiled. His chiseled figure towered over the room magnificently. His bright eyes sparkled at the secretary whose mouth dropped open rather unprofessionally.

Possibly seeing the reflection of her stupefied face in Alexander's immaculate smile, Patty composed herself. "Can I help you, sir?"

"My name is Alexander Machomole, I am here to see the president."

Patty bolted straight up. "Mr. Machomole! The president wants to speak to you right away. Everyone is trying to see him, but he said he only wants to see you." She looked at Alexander from head to toe and back up, nodding with pressed lips as she did, as if to say, 'I can see why he wants to see you'.

"Quiet as you go in, sir," she said. "He's on an important call at the moment." She held a finger to her lips as she softly opened the grand wooden door.

Alexander stepped through to the president's office. It smelled of power and history. Every piece of furniture was of ancient hardwood and leather that was polished to an unnatural shimmer. The president labored through a phone call behind a grand desk in an even grander swiveling chair.

Alexander slipped flat against the wall by the door with his hands clasped in front of him and his head tilted down. His body language attempted to convey that he was not intently listening to the president's phone call, though he most certainly was.

"Look, your majesty, there are no aliens. There have never been any aliens, and if there were aliens, then I would call you and tell you all about them. Ok? Alright, I have to go now, King Pottlefoot. Okay, and a blessed Chichneehotle to you too. Bye-bye, now." The president hung up the phone and let out an exasperated groan. "Alexander, sit your pretty self down. I have a mission for you."

Alexander looked up at the sound of his name as though he had not been intently listening to the president's phone call. "Of course, Mr. President." He dutifully walked to the empty chair in front of the president's desk and sat down.

"That was the king of Urquanchanstan," the president said. "He seems to be reading too many fantasy novels lately. Believes aliens have landed in the middle of the night." The president eyed Alexander carefully, waiting for a response.

Alexander chuckled politely. "Well, that's ridiculous, sir."

The president stood abruptly with a mountain of fury. "Well, it's the goddamn truth!" He shouted before regaining his composure and sitting back down. "Sorry. My temper has been getting the better of me lately." He held down a button on a telecom microphone. "Hey Patty, sweet cheeks, order me another book on meditation, please." He released the button and sat far back in his chair, staring at Alexander.

Alexander, usually quite sure of himself, did not know how to respond. "Sir, are you telling me that aliens landed?"

"They sure did," he started casually, "and I've been telling everyone in the goddamn world that they haven't!" His voice had gone up like an escalator, and by the end of the sentence, he was standing again with his eyes bulging out. "Sorry, sorry." He sat back down looking disappointed. "Everybody saw the spaceship land, but I told them it was just a meteor. We're playing this close to the vest. I need you to go to the landing site and capture the alien. You think you can do that for me?"

Alexander jumped at the opportunity to be the hero but overshot his mark. "Sir, I can do anything," he said with as much stoicism as he could.

"You're an arrogant bastard, Alexander, but you're the best we've got. Listen, this is beyond classified. You can't let anyone know about your mission. You will find this alien and bring him to me." His voice was rising yet again. "I don't care if he's dead or alive, you bring him to me and don't let a f…" The president sputtered and clutched his throat, having stretched the volume of his voice beyond what his body could handle. The spasm in his jaw brought his voice down to a whisper. "There is a helicopter waiting on the roof. Now get out of here." He rubbed his throat with one hand and gestured to the door with the other.

Alexander stood and posed triumphantly with his chest out and fists balled at his sides. "I will not let you down, Mr. President."

"Go!" The president tried to yell but hoarsely whined instead. He gave another angry shooing motion toward the door. Alexander nodded and obliged, walking with an air of extraordinary self-assuredness. He swung the door open to the secretary who smiled dreamily at him. He strutted towards her and leaned over her desk. An angry whine shouted from a speaker in between them. "Alexander, get your butt to the roof!" There was a brief pause before a less angry whine continued. "Sugar muffin, could you be a doll and get me a hot water with lemon?" The speaker shut off.

Alexander grinned. "Sounds like we both have places to be. I'll catch you around, toots." He winked at Patty and turned swiftly around to strut out the door.

CHAPTER SEVEN

Sunlight pierced the window of the Chateau Marvaloo onto Charlando's potato-like face and stirred him from his slumber. He wriggled under the weight of his big, fluffy comforter, churning up rippling waves across the sea of blankets. The muffled voice of Mr. Hinkle called from the shore. "Good afternoon, Charlando. How are you feeling?"

Charlando bolted straight up, his squat torso poking out of the thick white sheets like a hairy mole on the face of an angel. "What time is it?" he shouted. "I need to get a sandwich for Janet!" He looked around the luxurious room in a panic.

"No need to worry," Mr. Hinkle replied. "It's noon, the perfect time for lunch. And guess what? I got every sandwich in town while you were sleeping!" He gestured excitedly to two carts stuffed with bags and covered plates.

Charlando sat in awe of the cornucopia before him. He didn't know what he was looking at, but it smelled of heaven. Neither did he know what noon was and could only assume that it was good too. Charlando's stomach growled demandingly at the food. "Do you think Janet would mind if we sampled the sandwiches?"

"She would think that was a great idea! Have as much as you'd like!" Mr. Hinkle lifted one of the plate-covers revealing a steaming pile of pastrami. The vapors floated up in a twirling stream, twisting and turning until touching the tip of Charlando's sniffing nostrils. The big fluffy sheets flew to the ceiling as Charlando lunged for the pastrami. Bits and pieces scattered across the room as he ravaged sandwich after sandwich. Wild cries of ecstasy abounded until, in recognition that there were no more sandwiches to be devoured, Charlando fell backward in a glutenous stupor.

"Did you enjoy them, Charlando?" Mr. Hinkle asked, his face sprayed green with bits of lettuce.

"They were wonderful," Charlando replied, glowing in a joyful daze. The intense satisfaction from his feast made him temporarily forget about Janet. He rolled deep into a dense mound of pillows at the end of the bed. Earth was such a beautiful place, full of the tastiest meats, the fluffiest bedding, and the kindest people. If only Janet was here to experience it with him. He hugged a pillow tight, imagining it to be Janet. Janet. "Janet!" he yelled. "What have I done? I ate all of Janet's sandwiches!" He sat upright on the bed and looked at Mr. Hinkle full of guilt and shame.

Mr. Hinkle looked back with an adoring smile. "Don't worry, Charlando. You need to eat too! We can go get Janet another sandwich. Was there one you liked best? We can get her one of those." Mr. Hinkle nodded excitedly.

"I suppose the one that was in the brown bag over there." Charlando pointed to what was left of a brown paper bag that he had torn to pieces and thrown aside in his shameless eating frenzy.

"Of course," Mr. Hinkle laughed. "No surprises there. That was from Big Bob's Sandwich Shop. He cares more about sandwiches than most people do for their own children."

"Will he make another for Janet?" Charlando asked. "If so, I will go with you. I would like to meet this Big Bob. He sounds like a remarkable human."

Mr. Hinkle laughed again. "I am sure he would love to meet you too!" He smiled for a moment before his face hardened to concern, a realization having befallen him. "Though I must warn you, he is not always a friendly man."

Mr. Hinkle led Charlando out of the hotel. The sun shone brightly from high in the sky. Charlando shielded his eyes from the light, feeling smart for finally foiling the sneaky sun.

A cab waited for them at the curb. Mr. Hinkle ushered Charlando inside. Charlando climbed through the door and felt his way across the seat suspiciously, this being the first time he had seen the inside of a car. Mr. Hinkle came in after him and helped Charlando get buckled.

"Where to?" The driver grunted. He peered in the rearview mirror at his passengers and jumped at the sight of Charlando. "Good lord, kid! What the hell happened to you?"

Mr. Hinkle exploded in defense of Charlando. "You look straight ahead, you freckled-faced freak!"

"Mr. Hinkle!" Charlando yelped.

"Wow man, I didn't mean to offend," the driver said sheepishly. "He's just the weirdest looking kid I've ever seen," he then mumbled to himself.

Mr. Hinkle's rage dissolved upon seeing Charlando's frightened face. "I'm sorry. I didn't mean to startle you. I was just trying to defend you from this mangy little miscreant." He turned to the cab driver. "The only thing that happened to Charlando was getting blessed with the visage of an Adonis," he snarked. "Now take us to Big Bob's on Bellington Street."

Charlando eyed the sharp lines on Mr. Hinkle's reddened face. He had never seen an angry person before and was deeply distraught by it. How can anyone be trusted if someone as nice as Mr. Hinkle could be so mean?

The car began moving, and the bustling city life passing by out the window drew Charlando's attention. How could there be so many people? He tried counting them but soon lost track. The buildings were endless too, and each lined with hundreds of windows. Could there possibly be enough people to fill them all?

The sights and sounds captivated Charlando all the way to the shop. They parked right outside, and the cab driver turned back to look at the two. Mr. Hinkle was quick to address him. "We'll be out in a few minutes. Keep it rolling." The driver sighed and turned around, grabbing a book from under the center console.

Mr. Hinkle gently tapped Charlando's shoulder, whose face and hands were glued to the window as he stared at the office building on the other side of the street. "We're here, Charlando," Mr. Hinkle said sweetly. "Are you ready to get Janet a sandwich?"

The word 'Janet' broke his stare. He turned excitedly. "Of course," he said, and the two got out of the cab.

The wide sidewalk was busy with people flying in every direction, effortlessly swerving around each other like a well-coordinated dance. Mr. Hinkle cut straight across in five easy strides. Charlando was flabbergasted at the speed of it all. He stood and watched until Mr. Hinkle gave him an encouraging gesture from the other side. Charlando closed his eyes and gave himself a silent affirmation. He opened his eyes and took a great waddle forward.

A fat man in a suit crashed into him hard. The onion-shaped Ooflan bounced off and rolled fully over his head and back onto his feet, where he promptly collided with a handsome hippy walking in the opposite direction. Charlando proceeded to roll around the sidewalk, bouncing off person after person until coming to a stop on his great round rear in the middle of the sidewalk.

Embarrassed beyond belief, Charlando swayed back and forth until he had enough momentum to swing to his feet. He then hobbled around the crowd to everyone he had hit and apologized profusely. Each person stood with a dumbstruck look on their face, accepting his apology with the utmost kindness. After finishing his apologies, Charlando shuffled over to Mr. Hinkle, who had been watching the event unfold with a look of terror on his face. "I'm sorry to keep you waiting," Charlando said to Mr. Hinkle.

"No need to apologize to me," Mr. Hinkle said as he grabbed Charlando by both shoulders. "Are you alright?"

"I think I may have made a fool of myself." Charlando's smile sagged, but Mr. Hinkle tousled his oily head and told him it was all okay. Charlando's face brightened, and they proceeded into the sandwich shop.

A bell tinkled as they stepped inside. The walls were pale yellow and without any decorations. Three tables were on the right side of the shop, with only a single chair each. "Big Bob is a bit strange," Mr. Hinkle said quietly, so only Charlando could hear. "It might be best if I do the talking."

"If you say so!" Charlando shouted back, not understanding the gesture.

A huge man dressed in camouflage barged out of a swinging door on the other side of a counter directly ahead of them. Mr. Hinkle stuck out his arm to stop Charlando from going forward. "What are you doing in my shop?" The big man asked aggressively, giving the two intruders a nasty, inquisitorial look

"My friend, we came for a sandwich," Mr. Hinkle said cautiously. Big Bob eyed him for some time before turning slightly and doing the same to Charlando. His face was unchanged when he saw Charlando, something no other human had yet managed; though his face, already so full of suspicion when looking at Mr. Hinkle, may not have been physically capable of contorting any further.

"You already got a sandwich today," Big Bob said gruffly. "One sandwich per day. No exceptions." He turned around and made to walk back out the swinging door but stopped at Mr. Hinkle's protest.

"Please, my friend, I am here to get a sandwich for someone else."

Big Bob turned around to face Mr. Hinkle once more. "And who might that be?" He leaned over the counter and stared searchingly into his eyes. "Tell me!"

"It is for Charlando, here," Mr. Hinkle replied quickly, putting an arm around him. "He is very hungry. I told him you are the best sandwich maker in the world, and he is dying to experience it for himself. Aren't you Charlando?" Mr. Hinkle nodded up and down in an attempt for Charlando to go along with his story, but Charlando just gazed back confused.

Big Bob was having none of it. "You tell me lies in my own shop!" His voice bellowed. "Begone, you filthy liar!"

Charlando waddled forward against the current of Big Bob's rage. "Wait, Mr. Bob! You are right, Mr. Hinkle was not being honest with you." He turned to look at Mr. Hinkle momentarily and continued. "And I'm not sure why. It was actually I who ate the sandwich you made earlier. The one you gave to Mr. Hinkle."

"Blasphemy!" Big Bob bellowed, but Charlando continued again with even more passion.

"That sandwich was the best thing I have ever known on this strange planet. The best thing apart from one. Her name is Janet, and it is for her that I come to you now. I meant to give her that sandwich, but somehow…" Charlando trailed off and hung his head low in shame.

"You ate the sandwich yourself," Big Bob finished for him. The anger had left him. He now sounded deeply empathetic. The story must have been quite relatable and moving, for, after a few moments of consideration, a tear rolled off his great stubbly cheek. "I will make you one more sandwich," Bob said with a voice quivering with emotion. "Maybe love will treat you with more kindness than it has me."

Charlando thanked him and watched him work, captivated by the display of mastery. Each movement was full of purpose and precision. Charlando gasped and Mr. Hinkle broke into applause after a particularly beautiful chop of an onion. Bob's artistry exceeded the highest of Charlando's dreams.

At last, Big Bob slipped the finished sandwich into a brown paper bag and placed it on the counter. "For Janet," he said, exhausted but at peace. Charlando waddled forward and took the bag. Big Bob smiled softly at Charlando.

"I appreciate this," Charlando said brightly. "If it is anything like the sandwich you made earlier, Janet will be very happy."

Mr. Hinkle chimed in too. "Thanks, Bobby. You make a mean sub."

Big Bob looked at him with disgust. "This sandwich is for Janet, you scamming sissy," he hissed. A moment later he noticed something at the entrance of the shop. His eyes bulged in fury. A crowd was peering in through the glass: all the people Charlando had bumped into, along with a handful of curious looky-loos not wanting to miss out on the fuss. "You dirty scoundrels are trying to trick me!" Big Bob was furious. "Get out, you gutless gimps! Get out!"

Charlando was too stunned to move. He racked his mind for what he did to offend Bob but could not think of anything. He would have much preferred to know what it was so he could apologize.

Mr. Hinkle was not as sentimental. He pulled Charlando to the door. "We got the sandwich, now let's get out of here!"

Big Bob boomed ballistically in retort, yelling unintelligible nonsense at a terrifying volume. Charlando could only wave politely in response as he was thrust through the shop door.

The door swung shut behind them. The crowd that gathered was very glad to see Charlando. They smiled and waved and generally seemed to wish goodwill upon him, but Mr. Hinkle seemed to recognize a danger unseen to Charlando. He cleared a path through the well-wishers and dragged him to the taxi waiting at the curb. He opened the cab door and hastily swept Charlando inside. "Take us back," Mr. Hinkle yelled to the driver.

The driver was not keen on taking such rudeness. He turned to face his passengers, using the front seat as leverage to get as close to them as possible. "You look here," he said to Mr. Hinkle, brandishing a small pistol. "You better tell me what you're up to or I'm calling the cops. I'm not your getaway driver. You hear? What's in that bag!"

Mr. Hinkle froze with his hands held high. "It's a sandwich! I swear, it's a sandwich!"

The driver was not impressed. He turned to face Charlando. He grimaced at the sight. "Show me," he said.

Though Charlando did not know exactly what the driver was holding, his intensity and the fear on Mr. Hinkle's face informed him somewhat of his peril. "I can show you," he said, pulling out the sandwich. "Mr. Bob made it for Janet. She is the love of my life. I met her last night in the park, and she asked me to get her one. Mr. Hinkle here was kind enough to get me a sandwich earlier, but it hurts to say, I ate it myself." Charlando deflated into his seat, squeezing thick ooze from his pores that wafted straight into the driver's face.

The driver softened his gaze and lowered his weapon. "This Janet must really be something special."

"She is," Charlando responded, springing back to life. "She is the most beautiful creature in all the universe, and it is my purpose in life to honor her."

"That's beautiful, Charlando. I'm sorry I almost shot you. You say this Janet is the most beautiful creature in the universe, but your heart is the most beautiful thing I've seen. Is there anything I can do to help you? I am afraid I don't have a purpose the way you do."

"But of course, you do, Mr. Driver man," Charlando said. "Love is the purpose of all things. That's what Mother always says. She sleeps in the bushes at the park."

"Your mother sounds like a very wise woman. I will have to think about that more. In the meantime, it would be an honor to drive you back to Janet. You said she was at the Chateau Marvaloo?"

"Thank you, Mr. Driver Man, but she is actually at the park. Could you take us there instead?"

"Of course," the driver kindly responded, and off they went. The driver whistled cheerful tunes as he drove, to which Charlando bobbed his head while gazing out the window. Mr. Hinkle stared straight into the seat in front of him, still petrified by the gun so recently shoved in his face.

Charlando asked Mr. Hinkle to stay by the cab while he found Janet, and Mr. Hinkle reluctantly agreed. Charlando felt relieved to be alone. The park was not as busy as the bustling sidewalk outside Big Bob's. A few people here and there were walking a dog or jogging in bright-colored spandex, but all were at a great distance apart.

He labored up the gently sloped path to the bench where he met Janet the night before. The thrill of seeing Janet again along with the strenuousness of the gentle slope left him panting hard. Beads of yellow Ooflan sweat rolled down his fat wrinkled head. His eyes burned from the bright afternoon sun beating down on him. The sandwich in his hand slapped his great round butt as his arm swung wildly with every pained waddle forward. Finally, hyperventilating and covered in yellow slime, he made it to the bench.

No one was there. He twirled around confused. An old lady was watching her ancient, little dog fertilize the great lawn. They both looked up at Charlando, disgusted by what they saw. The dog finished its business and they both walked away with upturned noses. Surely that was not Janet, Charlando thought.

In truth, Charlando couldn't remember what Janet looked like all that well. It had been dark when they met, and she was covered up quite a bit. However, that thought was too painful for Charlando to think. Instead, a crushing emptiness occupied his mind. He clutched the sandwich bag and lumbered to the bench. He rolled himself up to a seating position. His squat legs jutted straight off the edge. Without hesitation, he unwrapped the sandwich and swallowed each half whole. He sobbed.

CHAPTER EIGHT

Alexander spent the helicopter ride acknowledging his own importance. 'Savior of the World' was a fitting title, he thought. He could go with something that highlighted his extraordinary handsomeness, or sensational wit, but no. Though he was the best in so many ways, this was just in support of his true destiny. Everything clicked into place for him at the president's office. His remarkable physical and mental superiorities were bestowed upon him for one purpose: to save the world. He looked ahead to the pilot. Thank God he's a man, or he'd be back here begging me for marriage. We'd crash in a minute. He looked out at a whiff of clouds sailing in front of the sun. Sorry buddy, I'm the hottest thing in the sky today.

"We are two minutes out, soldier," the pilot said through their headphones. "Buckle your pretty butt in, or it'll be smeared on some rock down there."

Pretty indeed, Alexander thought. He buckled in just as the helicopter veered hard to the right. A few minutes later they touched down at a hidden helipad outside of town. A cab waited for him on the street. "You should be proud, son," Alexander said to the pilot as he stood to leave. "For generations, your kids will talk about how close you got to The Great Alexander, Savior of the World." He padded the pilot stiffly on the arm and leapt off towards the taxi.

Alexander graced the cab with his magnificent body. "Good afternoon," he said to the driver. "You are probably wondering who all this fuss is for. It is me, Alexander Machomole."

The driver did not immediately respond but instead finished reading the last few lines of the page he was on in his book. He then set it down and looked back at Alexander. "Where do you want to go?" he asked with none of the reverence Alexander had expected.

"You will take me to the town center," Alexander said curtly. The driver shifted into gear without responding and sped forward.

There were no other cars on the road into town, and the trees surrounding them gave an even greater sense of privacy. In combination with overwhelming grandiosity, this encouraged Alexander to be looser with the details of his mission than he originally intended. "You know that lady that called you? That was Patty Pickleson, secretary of the president." Alexander looked at the driver's unchanged expression in the rearview mirror. "As in *thee* president," he added.

The driver's eyes met Alexander's in the mirror for a few seconds before returning to the road. The need for recognition pushed Alexander further. "He gave me a mission. The president, I mean. Patty Pickleson is very much a woman and very much interested in me as well." Alexander smiled and raised his eyebrows, giving away how cool those words made him feel, but the driver showed no indication it was mutual.

"Do you speak English?" Alexander snarked.

"Of course. I spoke to you earlier," the driver calmly responded.

Alexander's lungs filled with breath of hot fury. How dare a filthy cab driver undermine the savior of the galaxy! Alexander unleashed the hot air in a spray of fiery spittle. "I know this might not sound important to you, a worthless pile of nothing, but I have been sent by *thee* president to find and capture an *alien* who landed in *your* disgusting town! So, unless your life includes harrowing tales of saving the universe from aliens, then shut your filthy, worthless mouth!" Alexander shut his mouth and nodded to himself feeling as though he had made quite an irrefutable point.

The cab driver looked briefly back into the mirror with a curious look on his face. "Did you say you are trying to find an alien?"

"I most certainly did, you pedestrian poophead."

"You know, I met an alien earlier today," the cab driver said with a broad, pleasant smile. "He looks a bit like a fat kid that fell in a hot vat of donut glaze, but he's the sweetest creature I've ever met. Ha! Maybe he did fall in a hot vat of donut glaze!"

Alexander was quite shocked to hear about this encounter. Surely this was the alien he was after. At the same time, he thought, this was to be expected. After all, it was very wise of him to divulge all the top-secret details of his mission to the first civilian he encountered. Yes, he thought. It was very wise and very prudent as well.

"Tell me, filthy cab driver, where did you meet this fat deformity?"

"Are you talking about Charlando, the alien?"

"Of course, I'm talking about the alien, you dimwitted dung-eater."

"Oh gosh, what a story. Well, I picked him up at the Chateau Marvaloo of course. He's staying there with his friend Mr. Hinkle. I don't care much for him, but if he's a friend of Charlando…"

"Good grief, will you shut your mouth, you filthy foreigner!" Alexander grabbed his temples to relieve himself of the pain brought on by the annoying driver's ramblings. "You said Chateau Marvaloo? Take me there and for the love of God don't speak again." Alexander exhaled audibly and laid down in the back seat, exhausted by the conversation.

CHAPTER NINE

Janet scraped her last bit of stale bread against the sides of a nearly empty bowl of soup. Though it was bland and from a questionable source, she wished there was more. Besides sustenance, eating provided an obvious course of action. Without a clear directive, her mind was free to wander to places her heart dared to dwell.

The morning, though full of disappointments, had provided the kind of clear-cut path on which Janet thrived. She awoke on a park bench deep into the morning and naturally figured she should walk home. Upon finding her former home reduced to a pile of rubble and surrounded by police, she decided to clear the area. Though she did not remember the night before, she assumed crossing the police line covered in ash and smelling like alcohol was a bad idea. With nothing but hunger to guide her, she made her way to a soup kitchen downtown, where she presently sat trying to decide what to do next.

Decisions were rarely clear for Janet. She could muse indefinitely on even the most mundane and straightforward issues, reaching deeper levels of understanding than others would even guess exist, though she seldom dove to these depths since her parents' passing. Without taking the time to engage in deep thought, her mind was filled with fragmented lines of reasoning that held no practical use. She might have been the smartest person in the world given time to think, but she was dumb as dirt in her daily dealings. Her intelligence only showed itself in the extent to which she knew herself to be an idiot.

Janet looked around. The tables were crowded with dusty people devouring their rations. Most were alone and quiet, but a table of six chatted gleefully. They didn't seem to notice the filthy man yelling nonsense to himself at the next table. They must have seen and heard him so many times that he slipped into the background. Janet did this with people on the street, but it was jarring to see one sitting inside at a table eating food. She could never stand watching her parents eat. Not seeing them as real people was the easiest way to make sense of their condition, but when they were eating, that was impossible.

Janet stood at the recollection of her parents. Urgency to leave tugged hard in her chest. The room became unfocussed except the exit which glowed ever so slightly. Her feet took commands from something other than her conscious mind, something secretive and dark that did not want Janet to think about certain things and would gladly eliminate all thoughts if necessary. Janet bolted out the door.

The streets were cast half in shadow by the falling sun. Janet sped through the shadow, searching. At last, a grocery store gleamed on the lit side of the street. She stopped to wait for a free path between the passing cars.

Something light and pointy plopped on her head. “Good afternoon, Janet,” it said. Janet jolted and swatted at the friendly bird. It fluttered into the air and hovered above her head just out of reach of Janet’s flailing. “Stop! It’s me, your friend! Remember?”

“I don’t have friends,” screeched Janet as she continued her waving.

“I thought you said I was your friend!”

“What are you talking about?” Janet stopped twirling and looked up at the bird. It bobbed up and down twice more before landing on her forehead. It looked down into Janet's crossed eyes. “Oh. It’s you.”

“I thought you would be happier to see me. Am I interrupting something important?”

“No, no. I was just going to go to that store over there. I need some, uh, stuff.”

“Mhm.” The bird looked up to the store and stared. “You know, I had a friend who got a taste for bread. She kept going to the same spot where an old man would toss it. I told her she needed to eat more seeds, get some berries one of these days, but she didn’t listen. Next thing I know, she’s going to restaurants and swooping at people’s plates when they weren’t looking. She’d get her bread and a bit more than that. She didn’t know what she was eating half the time. Until one day, she swooped down for a mouthful and ate her own cousin.” The bird looked down at Janet’s crossed eyes yet again. “You aren’t going to get bread, are you?”

“I wasn’t planning on it, no.”

“You know my story was a metaphor for alcohol, right?”

“Ahh. I did not know that. In that case, yes. I am going to get a lot of bread.” Janet saw an opening in the traffic and sped forward. The bird slid off her forehead but steadied quickly and flew tight circles around her while she walked.

"Think about what you are doing, Janet. You have so much to offer the world. To throw it away like this is a travesty!"

Janet stopped walking and turned to the sky. "I have nothing left to give. I gave it all and got nothing back. The world took my family and friends and house. It took my money, my dignity. What could I possibly still have that the world wants?"

"You don't have any money?"

"The world wants more money from me? You are a twittering twat." Janet spat on the ground and made again for the store.

"No, Janet! I only asked because you said you are going to buy bread! I was confused!"

"I never said I was going to *buy* anything." A knot formed in her stomach as she spoke, slowing her pace.

"Thievery? Surely not, Janet. You're a good person. Swindling the fine people of Gopher's Grocery is not what a good person would do."

Janet stopped walking and watched the bird buzz around her. "I don't know where you got the idea that I was a good person, or that I would be willing to do whatever you want me to do, but you should double check your sources. I drink bread, that's what I do. I don't need to necessarily, but I want to. I don't really want to either to be honest, but I can't stop myself from doing it, and I don't see the difference. Do you think I want to go in there and rob that place? Those poor, happy people terrified for their lives as I barge in and grab the biggest bottle of bread I can carry. Cops come in and try to tackle me, but I slash them with my bread bottle and anyone else who stands in my way. You think I want all of that?"

A little boy yelped from a few feet away and hid behind his parent's sheltering arms.

"The ugly lady said mean things, mommy!"

"It's okay, Jeramiah. The witch lady won't hurt you," the young mother said before casting an evil eye towards Janet and ushering her family into the store.

Glass doors slid shut behind them. Standing right where the mother disappeared was Janet's reflection. Her pink pajamas hung on her slouched body in pitiful fashion. Dirt and ash frizzed her hair to a gravity-defying nest atop which stood the finch. Her outline was menacing, but her eyes, wide as an owl's, were that of a frightened little girl.

The bird tapped its foot gently on Janet's head. "Turn around, Janet. There is somewhere I want to show you."

"I need bread," she answered feebly.

"You will never need bread again if you turn around now and do as I say."

Janet considered the bird's proposal. She had tried so many times to stop on her own without any success at all. For her to be able to stop now was the most absurd thing she could ever believe, and yet her desperation was just strong enough to try. There was no reason at all to trust this bird other than the fact she had no other choice. "Okay," she said. "Let's go."

The bird led Janet out of the parking lot and towards the edge of town. They walked for hours. Each passing block grew taller and more numerous trees and smaller and fewer buildings. A single farmhouse hid amongst the trees at the last cross street before the forest surrounding the city began in earnest. The last glow of the day dimmed in the west. A nearly full gibbous moon glowed in the gap between two sycamores to the east. To the north the paved road turned to dirt and rock. Janet stopped at the edge of the forest and looked up to the bird for answers.

"Don't worry. It's just a little bit farther," it said.

The pair continued down the moonlit road. The city disappeared entirely after a single swerve of the path. The forest was dark and silent, but its mighty power tingled an undefined sense, alerting all to the life brimming within. It was raw and unforgiving. Janet would not have felt safe without the woodland guide perched on her head.

In short time, Janet's senses adjusted to the subtle sights and sounds of the wild night. The rustling and buzzing and chirping harmonized perfectly. She recognized her trampling brought discord to the gentle song and lightened her steps accordingly. Her breath deepened until her chest was still and only the very bottom of her belly rose and fell to the rhythm of the forest.

They came to a stop at a fork in the road. The moon was high enough in the sky for Janet's adjusted eyes to see quite some way down the main road. It looked just as the rest of the forest, and she would have been content to continue down it at the bird's suggestion. Experiencing the serenity of the forest, she decided, had been sufficient reason for the bird to take her down this path.

The alternate path was a touch slimmer and curved quickly down to the left. A faint orange light glowed beyond the bend. Upon seeing it she realized her view of the rest of the forest was in black and white. She looked up to the bird who peeked back at her over her forehead. "Thank you for taking me here," she said.

"Do you know where you are?" the bird asked.

"I know that I feel better, and I'm not sure the other details of the location matter nearly as much."

"I hope that remains true. I am glad you are feeling better now, though I admit that was not my intent."

"You didn't want me to feel better? What's wrong with you?"

"No, no, Janet. I am very happy you are feeling better. I only meant that I intended this path to provide more lasting solace. Enjoying the moment is what we all strive for, but we carry the weight of the past wherever we go. Living in a way we are happy to remember is the only path to freedom from the tethers of anguish."

"So, I won't keep feeling good if I keep walking this path?"

"This path? Heavens no! You'll be eaten alive by the morning! I'm surprised you made it this far, to be honest. This place is a death trap. A pack of wolves has been following you for an hour. I'm shocked you kept going after all the howling."

"I thought that was the peaceful song of the forest?"

"That was the dinner bell, that was. I would run towards that light if I were you, Janet."

A wolf growled behind them. Another joined from ahead. A third made Janet turn to the right. Two yellow eyes appeared out of the darkness between the trees. Sharp fangs glistened in the moonlight right below them.

"Run, Janet, run!"

Janet squealed and ran down the curved path. The bird fell off her head and flew up to the trees and out of sight. The path curved quickly again to the right and opened to a clearing. The orange light came from a network of log cabins laid out before her. She ran to the closest one and banged on the door. "Help! Help!" she yelled. She turned her back to the door and braced for the approaching wolves.

She heard nothing but the sound of her heavy breathing. The wolves would be surrounding her now. She was trapped. Janet pitied herself for all days she could have gone without drinking, it was the one where she gets eaten by wolves. Maybe being eaten by wolves was the only way she could get through an entire day. Maybe that's how the bird would keep its promise.

Just as all hope was lost, the door behind her creaked open. Janet yelped and spun around to face the sound. A wall of warm air and soft light hit her face. The young hippy woman from the day before stood inside the doorway. Her eyebrows were stretched halfway to her hairline.

"Hello," she said kindlier than Janet expected. "Did you walk here?"

"Oh, hello. I walked for most of it, but I ran the last little bit."

"I see that. Do you want to come in?" The young woman said. She stood to the side to allow Janet passage.

"Yes, please," Janet responded before leaping into the cabin. The warmth emanating from a crackling fire on the left side of the room enveloped her right away. Two rustic couches sat atop a large furry rug on either side of the fireplace. Between the couches was an oval, wooden table. The walls were decorated with a patterned quilt and paintings of landscapes and people and abstract designs. Potted house plants dotted every available corner. On the right side of the room was a door to a kitchen and straight ahead was a hallway leading to two bedrooms, a bathroom, and another door to the outside. "Your house is really nice," Janet said.

"Thank you, but it's not actually mine. I have the van outside. This belongs to Richard and his friends."

"Who's Richard?" Janet asked.

"He's the guy you were talking to yesterday. He's in the next cabin drinking and playing music with the rest of them. That's pretty much all they do. I'm Merideth, by the way." Merideth held out a hand to Janet.

Janet looked skeptically at Merideth's gesture for a second before reaching out her own hand. "I'm Janet," she said. "It's nice to meet you."

"It's nice to meet you too, Janet. Do you want to sit by the fire? You look a little chilly. I can get you some coffee or hot chocolate if you want." Merideth directed Janet toward the couches.

"You have hot chocolate?" Janet asked, still surprised by Merideth's hospitality.

"Yeah, why not? Here, take a seat. I'll be back in a minute."

Merideth left for the kitchen. Janet sat on the couch facing the hung quilt. It was far more comfortable than it looked, though her sticky pink pajamas made it hard to enjoy it fully. She looked into the fire, whose radiance felt like it might singe her frizzy hair. It looked just like the fire that burned down her house the night before, just locked in a cage. It was beautiful and calming right where it was, but just three feet to the right and the same fire would be a disaster. It was hard to believe one thing's nature could have such divergent implications in applications so narrowly dissimilar.

Merideth walked back into the living room with two mugs of hot chocolate. She placed one on a coaster in front of Janet and sipped the other while making her way to a seat on the couch opposite her. She sat cross-legged and smiled. "So, what brought you here?" she asked.

"Well," Janet began, but did not finish. She looked up to a corner of the ceiling, searching for a place to start in her story that would not require further explanation. Following the advice of a bird was not that. "I burned my house down last night," Janet said, though it did not fit the criteria either. "It was an accident, but I don't have anywhere else to go and I just happened to stumble across this place. Another accident, I guess, but a good one. Thanks again for letting me in."

Merideth smiled sympathetically at Janet and nodded her head. "I guess that explains why you're wearing the same clothes as yesterday and smell like smoke. I have some extra clothes you can have. We have a shower too. You should really take a shower."

"Thank you," Janet replied, embarrassed. She looked down at her pink pajamas and grimaced. They, much like the fire, gave a different impression than the day before.

"You were pretty drunk yesterday. Is that why you burned your house down?" Merideth calmly took another sip of her hot chocolate waiting for an answer.

Janet's eyes bulged. "You knew I was drunk?"

"Are you kidding? You were hammered, and it was the morning too. You didn't finish that entire bottle in your bag, did you? I guess that would be enough to accidentally burn your house down."

Janet's mouth gaped and her cheeks turned pale. The coziness of the cabin was gone. Her secret life was ripped open and exposed.

"I didn't mean to offend you. It was just really obvious yesterday and you're not drunk now, so I thought I'd ask. You don't have to tell me if you don't want to."

Janet leaned back on the couch and thought about the night before. She hadn't explicitly blamed her drinking for the fire, although it was hard to deny now that the idea was presented. It was a disturbing revelation to make the connection between her drinking and any one event that happened in her life. Deep down she knew she was worse off for her addiction, but the regularity with which she drank made it impossible to know who she was and how her life would go without alcohol. This lack of a benchmark made it easy to underestimate the severity of her problem. Merideth's question blew the doors off the house of illusions.

Janet's eyes darted around the room synchronously with her mind's eye, which searched her brain for something to say. Merideth relieved her of the task.

"I wasn't doing too well when I came here either. I didn't have a drinking problem, more of a generalized spiritual crisis, but I know what it's like to not have anywhere to go or anyone to turn to. I ran away from home when I was 16. My dad left my mom when I was a baby and she blamed me for losing him. Maybe it was because of me, but then again, I left her the moment I got the chance too. She's cool when she has control over everything, but she's cruel if you show any autonomy. If my dad is anything like me, then I imagine that's the real reason he left. Who knows?"

Janet shrugged while keeping her gaze glued to the fire.

"Anyways, I took a van that my dad left at the house and drove around the country looking for a place to live. I was on the road for three years and never felt like I was home. Then I drove into this forest. Something about it felt like I was where I belong. I drove down that driveway thinking it would be a good place to park for the night. I saw the cabins and thought I would have to turn around and find another place, but Richard came out and stopped me. He asked if I needed a place to stay and said he had a free room. He kicked his friends out of this cabin and let me spend the night. I've been here for two years now. He can be a pretty nice guy."

"Are you guys a couple now?" Janet asked. Somewhere in Merideth's story, Janet stopped thinking about herself.

"Richard and I? Definitely not. He hit on me a lot when I first moved here, and I thought he was pretty cute, but then I realized he does that with every girl he meets, and it lost its charm. He wrote me a song that almost made me fall for him, but not quite. I made him record it. Do you want to hear it?"

"Yes, please!"

Merideth excitedly set down her mug and sprung up to a short bookshelf next to her couch. The top shelf was lined with records, which she thumbed through before pulling out one with a homemade cover. She pulled out the record and placed it on a record player sitting on top of the shelf. She turned swiftly around to Janet. "You ready?"

Janet nodded up and down vigorously. Merideth turned back around. She gently lifted the needle into place. The speaker crackled and popped for a couple of seconds before an acoustic guitar came in. It played simple chords but with a gently swinging fingerpicking style that gave texture and melody. After a full run through of the main chords, a strong but vulnerable voice sang over the same progression.

Down the road
Something's comin' near
It's quite distinct
Not by sight nor ear
You can tell right away
You ain't smellin' no skunk
That's a different kind of animal
That's little hippy funk

Little Hippy
Living in a van
Trying her hardest
The best she can
She's a wishin' and a prayin'
Hoping no one can tell
But you just can't hide
That little hippy smell

Little hippy
Don't be ashamed
You light up my life
Bright as a flame
'Cause inside you

Stronger than any fart
Is the beat, beat, beat
Of the little hippy heart

The music stopped, and the speaker crumpled for another second before Merideth turned it off and returned the record to its jacket.

"That was amazing," Janet said.

Merideth laughed. "I thought so too. Then about the twentieth time I listened to it, I realized he was just telling me I smelled bad." She laughed again even harder.

Janet laughed too, something that minutes before seemed impossible. "I guess that could be true, but I don't think you can write such a beautiful song about someone you don't think is beautiful."

"Thank you. He must see beauty in a lot of things then. That actually does sound like him."

"Interesting. I still don't get why you're not together."

Merideth laughed again. "He's a good guy. He's the best guy, really, but he's just a friend. I feel better when I'm alone, anyways."

"That makes sense. I spend pretty much all my time alone. I'm not sure if it's by choice or not, though." Janet stared at her feet, thinking hard about her social life.

Merideth set her mug down and unfolded her arms. She leaned forward and looked at Janet like she was solving a puzzle. "You're a weird girl," she said.

Janet looked up. She was not offended by being called 'weird', rather comforted that someone was acknowledging something she knew to be true about herself.

"And you are definitely choosing to be alone," Merideth continued. "There are plenty of people who would want to spend time with you, you just don't want to be around them. It's a mistake, too. Just because you want to be alone doesn't mean you won't get lonely."

Merideth stopped talking for a moment. Janet squirmed a little but didn't respond. She had not talked to anyone for a long time, and maybe never to someone as perceptive as Merideth. She wondered how quickly Merideth could know something about her that she could not figure out in 22 years.

"You don't talk much," Merideth said. "I like that about you, but it's also a bit frustrating."

"I'm sorry," Janet said.

"Don't be sorry, I just said I like you. I can tell there's a lot going on in your mind. The most interesting people seem to say the least about themselves. It's like you're guarding some secret treasure."

"Well, you're interesting, and you talk a lot about yourself," Janet countered.

Merideth fell back on the couch laughing before collecting herself and standing up. "Thank you, Janet. I'm going to go to sleep now. I'll put some clothes in the bathroom for you, if you could please take a shower. It's the first door on the right. The room on the left is empty. You can sleep in there. And help yourself to anything in the kitchen. Maybe you can find something you like better than cold hot chocolate."

"Thank you," Janet said. "You are very kind."

"Like I said before, this place isn't mine. Anyways, good night, Janet."

"Good night, Merideth."

Merideth grabbed her empty mug and dropped it off in the kitchen sink before heading down the hall. Janet could hear her drop off the clothes in the bathroom and brush her teeth before finally shutting her bedroom door.

The night again was quiet except the popping of the smoldering fire. Janet reached for her hot chocolate and took her first sip. It had indeed gone cold, but tasted delicious nonetheless. She sat back on the couch and watched the last remnants of logs reduce to glowing coals.

The long day weighed heavily on her eyelids. She thought about Merideth's journey in her van, and how much she would like to know more about what she saw. Unlike the anxious direction her consciousness usually took, these thoughts were comforting and made her feel whole. The comfort was enough to sink her into a deep sleep, where she dreamed of her new friend.

CHAPTER TEN

Charlando tossed and turned in the king bed of his luxury suite at the Chateau Marvaloo. The big fluffy sheets wrapped around him as he rolled about. Tighter and tighter, the sheets constricted. In his dreams, he was big and strong and light of foot, chasing a faceless woman whose laugh echoed just out of reach. In the waking world, Charlando was a fat potato goblin, immobilized by a satin swaddle.

His eyes opened to the bright light of day. He wobbled in his cocoon but quickly gave up on breaking free. There was no freedom from the void crushing him from within. He stared straight ahead at the floor-to-ceiling window on the other side of the room. The hotel across the street sparkled: a wall full of people who could do nothing to take his loneliness away. He felt just as he had years before, staring out a tiny window at empty space. There were billions of miles between him and anyone else at that time. There was a good reason for the loneliness he felt then. What was the reason now?

"Good morning, Charlando," Mr. Hinkle blurted out upon seeing the whites of Charlando's eyes. He stood feet away holding a tray of pastries. "I brought you some breakfast." He held out the tray for Charlando to see.

The sweet smell tugged hard on Charlando's empty stomach. He gyrated like a maraca until the seams of his cocoon burst. He flopped to Mr. Hinkle and ravaged the flaky delights. Mr. Hinkle struggled to keep the tray aloft.

Charlando sucked up the last crumbs of streusel and collapsed back on the bed. "Thank you," he muttered before curling into a motionless ball.

"You're very welcome," Mr. Hinkle said. "Is there anything else I can get for you? You seem a bit sad."

"No, thank you, Mr. Hinkle. I am afraid there is nothing that can be done. I would just like to be left alone."

"Oh, Charlando. You *are* sad! You can talk to me about it, you know?" Mr. Hinkle set the tray on a desk and sat beside Charlando on the bed. He rested a hand on Charlando's back. "Tell me what's troubling you."

"It's nothing, really. I just don't know what to do about Janet." Charlando scooched ineffectively away from Mr. Hinkle's hand, not appreciating the touch.

"Oh, I think you should forget about that girl," Mr. Hinkle scooched himself closer and pressed his hand more firmly. Charlando again tried and failed to wiggle away. Mr. Hinkle responded by making circular massaging motions. "Everything will be alright, Charlando. I always thought Janet was a real bimbo anyways, sending you to get her a sandwich. What a tramp."

Charlando spasmed violently, knocking Mr. Hinkle's hand away and flipping himself to a crouched position in the middle of the bed. "Janet is the most beautiful person in all the world!" Charlando wailed. "And I said leave me alone! If you don't like Janet, then I don't want you around. Now get out!"

Mr. Hinkle stood with his palms out apologetically. A panicked look was plastered on his face. "I didn't mean it," he pleaded, but Charlando did not want to hear it.

"Get out!" He belched out one last time. Mr. Hinkle regretfully conceded and backed out of the room, quietly pleading for forgiveness.

Charlando stayed squatting temperamentally on the bed until his thighs seared with fatigue. He fell back on his great, round rump and flailed like a tortoise flipped on its shell. After a minute of waving about, hopelessness paralyzed the potato goblin.

Charlando could stare at the ceiling no more. How long had passed, he did not know. It could have been days or years. The sun shone in nearly the same place, though maybe this was just another trick by the sneaky sun. It was not. He had been on his back for only a few minutes.

All at once, the energy from three dozen pastries surged through Charlando. He swayed from side to side in bigger and bigger arcs until a great heave took him to the brink of freedom. He balanced precariously, desperately waving his free hand to usher himself forward. With a triumphant plop, he flopped onto his stomach and off the bed. The floor was much harder and easier to transverse. He easily rocked himself to a standing position and from there, waddled out the door.

He passed by Mr. Hinkle, who was keeping post outside. "Charlando!" Mr. Hinkle called out, surprised. Charlando did not respond, but instead hardened his expression and waddled with more determination to the elevator. He stood and stared at the metallic doors. His confusion reflected back at himself.

"Press the button with the downward arrow," Mr. Hinkle whispered cautiously.

Charlando turned his head and frowned at Mr. Hinkle before pressing the button. A light blinked above him, and shortly after, the metallic doors slid open. Charlando walked inside and turned around. He saw a grid of buttons on each side of the door and his eyes widened with fear. The doors began to close.

Mr. Hinkle yelled desperately. "Press the 'L'! Press the 'L'!"

Charlando panicked. He scanned the buttons, but the illiterate Ooflan had no hope of finding the letter 'L'. He despaired, unsure of the consequences of pressing incorrectly. Just when his hopelessness became unbearable, the doors slid open again. Mr. Hinkle was there mouthing the word 'L' and drawing it in the air for Charlando. Charlando recognized the motion and turned back to the grid of buttons. There it was at the very bottom. He pressed it with his grubby finger and scornfully looked back up to Mr. Hinkle as the doors closed. He would have to do more than that to return to Charlando's good graces.

The elevator began to fall and Charlando gripped the railing tight. For a moment he felt as light as he did in the spaceship, but as the elevator came to a stop on the bottom floor, Charlando felt heavier than ever, both physically and emotionally. He bolted out of the elevator as soon as the doors opened. He did not know where he was going, but the drive to escape his feelings propelled him as though he was in a great rush.

A few guests patrolled the lobby. All of whom, apart from a young girl, towered over Charlando. Each one that noticed Charlando balked and stared. Behind the concierge desk stood the same set of beautiful young women who were there the day before.

Two of them laughed out loud upon seeing Charlando, and the third appeared to throw up in her mouth. They then turned to each other and began whispering, all at the same time and at speeds only young women can understand.

Charlando stopped waddling and stared at the girls. He looked around at all the people's disgusted faces and then something else caught his eye. Reflected in a decorative mirrored wall beside him, stood a short, slimy, fat, disgusting, potato goblin. "There is no way," he said to himself. He again looked around the room at all the beautiful faces staring at him. Again, his eye caught sight of a hideous slime monster, now reflected in the butt of a well-polished statue of a nude man. He waddled to the statue and stared into its butt. He touched his face and saw the grotesque creature in the butt do the same. "Oh no," he cried to himself. "I'm fat and hideous." He looked down at his protruding belly and cried.

The little girl in the lobby snuck away from her parents as they spoke to one of the women behind the concierge desk. She crept across the lobby to Charlando. She tip-toed up curiously, and with the tactlessness customary of children, she poked him hard in his great, fat belly. Charlando flopped backward in terror and squealed as he landed on his spectacular rear.

The girl's parents turned to see their daughter pointing and laughing at the fallen Charlando. They hurried over to their daughter furiously. "Beatrice!" The mother screeched. "What are you doing to that poor, sick boy!" She grabbed Beatrice by the arm and turned her towards herself to better scold her.

Beatrice's father went to Charlando's aide. "Are you alright there, little fella," he said as he bent down to help Charlando up. He gasped when he got close enough to see the Ooflan up close but helped rock him to his feet regardless.

Charlando was too mortified to offer any response at all. His reflection brought about the realization that his loneliness would never be cured. Janet must not have seen him clearly the night they met, otherwise she would never have spoken to him. She must have seen him coming with the sandwich and realized she made a terrible mistake. No one could ever love such a hideous creature as himself. He wept passionately and inconsolably.

Beatrice's father, Tony, began crying too. He swallowed Charlando in a warm, fatherly hug and the two moaned in harmony, swaying to the sound of their own cries. "You poor, beautiful boy! Please be alright," Tony moaned.

Beatrice and her mother, Cassandra, turned to stare at the weeping odd couple. The rest of the lobby took notice. Some people inched closer to get a better view while others stared politely out of the corner of their eyes. The only sounds in the grand lobby were the tinkling of fountains and Charlando's and Tony's sonorous cries.

A ding came from the elevator and the doors slid open. Mr. Hinkle rushed out into the somber lobby. He saw Tony holding Charlando and exploded without any comprehension of the events that had just unfolded. "Get your hands off him!" He yelled and sprinted towards the crying couple. "I am coming, Charlando!"

The entire lobby, Charlando included, turned to look at Mr. Hinkle. His face was red and maniacal. His arms flailed above his head as though he were trying to scare off a wild animal stalking his child. Tony pulled Charlando behind him to shield him from the approaching maniac. He stood his ground and braced for the impending brawl.

Mr. Hinkle barreled into Tony. The impact knocked him back into Charlando. Tony sank into Charlando's protruding belly like a foot into a bouncy ball. Charlando's belly rebounded and sent him somersaulting backward through the air. He bounced to a stop on the ground a fair distance away. Mr. Hinkle and Tony tangled together and rolled across the lobby. Mr. Hinkle ceaselessly yelled out for Charlando's protection.

Anger supplanted the sadness in Charlando. "Stop!" he yelled at the top of his lungs. He could not see anything other than the painted ceiling above him but knew the two men stopped fighting at the cessation of Mr. Hinkle's war screams. All eyes in the lobby were back on Charlando. The slimy Ooflan rocked himself to his feet. He stared daggers at Mr. Hinkle. A tear dripped from his eye. "You have gone too far," he said. "I told you before to leave me alone, and now I mean it for good. I don't want to see you ever again!"

Charlando turned to the exit and waddled as fast as he could out the door. He bowled over several people on his way out but was crying too hard to apologize. Danny, the doorman, was standing outside. His smile faltered upon seeing Charlando's tears. "Charlando, what's wrong?"

Charlando paused and looked at Danny's friendly face. He began crying again and waddled in for a hug. "Oh, Danny," he said. "Everything is wrong. I saw myself in the butt and now Janet doesn't love me because I am fat and hideous. A little girl knocked me to the ground and Mr. Hinkle killed the man who helped me up!" Charlando cried deeper until his feelings were too much to handle. "I have to get out of here," he spurted out, and he turned away from Danny, waddling into the city.

The streets bustled with morning commuters. Charlando had never seen so many people or heard so many sounds. Music blared from cars stuck in traffic. Horns honked. Venders shouted. Hordes of people raced every which way down the crowded sidewalks. Charlando bounced amongst them like a pinball.

The hotel quickly disappeared behind the tall figures. There was no telling if he would ever make it back there. The will of the stream of pedestrians decided his destination, and he was okay with that. The food was tasty at the Marvaloo, but Mr. Hinkle was not worth the trouble. Besides, Janet would never love a potato goblin who does nothing but lay in bed eating streusel.

CHAPTER ELEVEN

A phone rang eighteen times on a bedside table before falling silent, untouched. Less than a minute later, the phone rang again. Alexander groaned. Who dares disturb the savior of the universe? He flipped onto his stomach and dragged the phone to his ear. "Who is this?" He muffled into his pillow.

"This is your president, you lazy mule!"

Alexander shot up to attention. "Mr. President, so good to hear from you. For what do I owe the pleasure?"

"You dirty son of a dog, you don't think I know what you're doing?"

"I'm capturing an alien Mr. President. Those were your orders, and let me assure you, I am laser focused. I am doing anything and everything to do so and nothing else. Capturing an alien is no easy task; that, I am sure, is why you entrusted it to me."

Just then, a woman in a revealing dress and heels walked out of the bathroom with her arms crossed and a dissatisfied look on her face. "Alien?" she mouthed. Alexander grimaced and shook his head. He pointed to the door with hope that she would leave. Her mouth fell open at the gesture. She snatched her bag from a dresser by the door and left the room in a huff, slamming the door behind her.

"Well, give me an update then," the president said. "Have you found it yet?"

"Of course I have. He's staying at the Chateau Marvaloo. I've been doing reconnaissance from the hotel across the street. He has the hotel staff under his control. He seems to have exceptional intellectual and persuasive abilities. I've only seen such skills in myself, to be honest. Sir, you made an excellent decision to give this task to me. I am afraid I am the only one who stands a chance."

"You let him take over the Chateau Marvaloo? Good God, you disgraceful idiot. Capture him today! You understand me, soldier?"

"Today? But Mr. President, I can't stress to you enough the detail and complexity of this mission."

"Just stuff him in a bag! Do it, or I'm putting Freddy on it!"

"Freddy?" Alexander objected, but the president had already hung up the phone.

Alexander slammed his phone down too. There was no way he would lose another mission to Freddy, Mr. Perfect Secret Agent Man, Jones. Freddy was off fighting in regular human wars. It was Alexander who was assigned to intergalactic combat. It was Alexander whose destiny it was to save the world from the evil aliens.

Alexander shot to the window overlooking the street, across which was the Chateau Marvaloo. He grabbed a pair of binoculars resting on a desk to the side of him. His vision narrowed on the alien's suite. The curtains were drawn, revealing not the gross little alien, but a middle-aged man weeping on the bed by himself. He rocked back and forth with his face buried in his hands. It was a pathetic sight that lasted several minutes.

Right as Alexander was about to take a break, the man on the bed turned suddenly to the door. He stood and yelled something. The door opened, and a room service attendant rolled in a cart filled with covered plates. The man did not seem happy with this. He waved furiously at the room service attendant who held up his hands and walked slowly out of the room before returning immediately with two more carts. One he pushed in front of him and the other he pulled behind. Both were stacked high with plates. The man seemed satisfied with this and directed the room service attendant out of the room. As soon as he left, the man's shoulders slumped. He staggered to the window and looked down to the street gloomily.

Alexander lowered his binoculars. Where was the alien? There was no way that Alexander could have missed him. He scanned the hotel again and then the street. At the very end of his line of sight he saw what he was looking for. Hidden in the crowd just down the street was a little tuft of onion hair bobbing up and down.

"I'm coming for you, alien," he said to himself. His low gravelly voice irritated his throat, throwing him into a coughing fit. He clutched his throat and clawed around for a bottle of water on the bedside table. A few sips settled the attack. "Right after I get myself a steaming cup of coffee," he continued to himself in his low, heroic voice.

CHAPTER TWELVE

Janet cut off a piece of French toast from a pile on a plate before her. She held it up to study. Its golden-brown exterior was leathery and dripping with gooey syrup. Its insides quickly transitioned to a yellow, spongy texture that lightened towards the middle. The center was a line of white, fluffy bread that appeared to get through the entire cooking process completely unscathed. It was like fossilized heat exchange.

"You really like French toast, huh?" Richard asked. He wore an apron with no trace of use, looking stylish even at home in the morning making breakfast.

Janet stuffed her mouth with the heaving fork right as the question was asked. She swallowed prematurely and choked. Water sloshed off the side of her cup as she grabbed it and guzzled, forcing the fluffy French toast down. She wiped her face of syrup and spilled water. "I've actually never had it before," she said, panting.

Merideth sat beside Janet, bûrying her face in her elbow to suppress her laughter. They both sat at a long wooden table in the main cabin of the commune. Janet slept well into the morning, so the rest of the members had already eaten and were off passing the time in other rooms and outside.

"You've never had French toast? What kind of neglected childhood did you have?" Richard asked. He smiled playfully, but the question stung. The truth was too complex to give a quick response, and Richard didn't wait for one. "My butler made it for me every morning. He used fresh brioche that puts this trash to shame. I think we need a bakery on the commune. What do you think, Merry?"

Merideth looked disgusted. "I think regular bread is just fine," she said.

"Just because you're a hippy doesn't mean you can't eat nice bread."

"I'm not a hippy, and I have eaten nice bread. The bread in your hands is nice. You don't need to build a bakery just to have French toast."

"Well, it wouldn't just be for French toast. We could bake buns and cook hamburgers and hotdogs. You don't want to have a party?" Richard pranced around while he talked like he was swaying to music only he could hear.

"You don't need to build a bakery to have a party. That makes no sense. Just buy some buns."

"Are you kidding me? You haven't had a hamburger until you've had it on a freshly baked bun. Tell her, Janet." Richard waved a spatula at Janet like a conductor.

Janet's mouth was again full of French toast, but having learned from her earlier mistake, she decided to chew it thoroughly before swallowing. Though she tried to chomp as quickly as possible, it seemed to take much longer than a normal bite. Maybe by concentrating on chewing, her chewing mechanics deviated from those subconsciously perfected over millions of chews. Janet tried pushing thoughts of masticating to her periphery to see if this would quicken her pace. To her surprise, it made her stop chewing altogether.

"Are you alright, Janet?" Meredith asked.

Janet's mind returned to the room. The French toast in her mouth was sufficiently soft and she swallowed. Richard and Merideth were both staring at her. "Yes," she said. "What was the question again?"

Meredith turned to Richard. "I don't think she cares about your bakery," she said. Her voice was apologetic, but the corners of her mouth tugged taught inwards and up, hinting of delight.

"Oh, the bakery!" Janet remembered, "I have never been to a bakery or a party, so I can't speak from experience about one's necessity to the other, but I could think about it if you like." She stared blankly for a moment. The idea is that one needs a bakery for a bun, a bun for a hamburger, and a hamburger for a party. But what about a search party? A hamburger would be helpful, but likely unnecessary for a search party. "I am leaning toward believing they are independent in their existence, but not so for their quality. I think you may have forgotten about search parties. Should we set up an experiment to be sure?"

Janet watched the corners of Merideth's mouth slump. Did she say something impolite? This was the most she had ever said to Merideth. It was the most she had said to anyone in many years, for that matter. She had not had this much to say nor anyone to say it to. Was it a coincidence this was also the first time in years that she was not even a little bit drunk? Was there a remedy for this close by?

Richard filled the silence with laughter. "I think you're right. Not all parties need bakeries, just the good ones. Thank you, Janet."

"You're welcome!" Janet replied enthusiastically, relieved to hear her statement was taken well.

Richard bounced his eyebrows twice at Merideth who rolled her eyes in response. This seemed to convey enough meaning to bring the debate of the bakery to a close. Richard triumphantly threw the spatula in the sink and grabbed his coffee off the counter to sip with the girls at the table. "So, you came for the meeting?" he asked. "I thought you wouldn't make it."

Janet recalled their conversation at the park. Had she given him a specific reason why she couldn't come? She could not remember. Lies are convenient until you see the person again. "Yes. I wasn't sure if I could make it either and I didn't want to make a commitment I couldn't keep."

"That's great! We're happy to have you," Richard said. He paused for a moment to look around the room and continued in a quieter voice. "To be honest, most of the people here are idiots. It's basically just the two of us that contribute, and I don't know how much longer Merry is going to stick around." He gave a downcast shrug and sipped his coffee. His big mug hid most of his face, but the crinkle of his eyes suggested he was not as worried as he let on.

Merideth shook her head. "He says things like that because he wants me to stay forever but is too scared to ask. It's pathetic, but I put up with it for the French toast."

Richard grimaced as though he had been kicked in the shin. "I have enjoyed and grown accustomed to your company, and it would be nice to know how much longer I will be enjoying it. I suppose maybe that is pathetic. I am sorry."

"It's too early for this," Meredith said irritably. "Janet, please don't take offense to this, but you really need to take that shower. I put some clothes in the bathroom for you already. You can use whatever you find in there."

Janet had forgotten that she had not showered in days. The reminder made her suddenly aware that her outermost layer of skin had been replaced with a thick layer of filth. An itch sprouted from the back of her head, and she scratched it instinctively. She stopped upon seeing the disgusted looks on her new friends' faces. "I'm sorry I'm gross. I will take a shower now." She stood up and grabbed her empty plate to take to the sink.

Richard stood up and reached for the plate. "I can take that for you, Janet," he said kindly.

"Thank you," Janet replied. She shuffled out of the room, closing the door gently behind her.

For a moment she had thought she was just a normal person having breakfast, but that was foolish. She did not belong with other people. She looked down at her clothes. They used to be a pretty pink. Now they looked like a used eraser. There is no erasing the truth, however. She buried the truth in the deepest depths of herself, and still it was only ever a few inches from the surface.

Janet heard Merideth and Richard voices return through the door. She leaned her ear against the space between the door and frame and listened closely.

"Man, that was pretty harsh," Richard said.

"I didn't mean it to be," Meredith replied. "I just couldn't take that smell anymore."

"Oh God, it's awful. Hey, does she really have to stay here?"

"Richard! I told you, she has nowhere else to go. I think once she takes a shower it'll be easier to talk to her. She actually seems smart in a weird way. She also seems like an idiot. I don't know what she is, but she's staying here until she gets back on her feet at least."

"Maybe she's more interesting after a couple drinks."

"No! Richard, I didn't say this before, and don't tell anyone else, but I think she's an alcoholic. She was so drunk on Saturday, and that was in the morning. And she told me that her house burned down that night, and that's why she doesn't have a place to live. I think she burned her house down because she was so drunk, and I think that's also why she's so weird. I also think that we need to be nice to her and make her feel welcome because she's fragile, and she doesn't have any family or friends. She is alone in the world. Be nice to her and don't drink around her at all. Okay?"

"Okay. Fine. I'll be nice to her, but you have to make her take a shower every day."

Janet pulled her head away from the door. There was no way she was staying long enough to take a shower. The small piece of herself she let slip to Merideth was tossed immediately to the wind.

Janet sped off down the hallway to Merideth's cabin. She flew by the bathroom and grabbed her purse from the table in front of the fireplace. She swung open the door to the outside and was hit directly in the forehead with a friendly finch.

"Where are you going in such a hurry?" the finch sang.

"I'm going away. I don't know why you brought me here, but it was a mistake for me to listen to you. You're a freaking finch for God's sake." Janet stormed out the door and onto the dirt road.

"Better a finch than a grinch!"

"You better shut your mouth. I was happy before you came along. I had a home. Now what do I have?"

"You have a different home!"

"That's not a home. They don't even want me there. They are letting me stay because they think I'm pathetic and need their charity."

"They sound like good, sensible people to me."

"So you're saying I'm some charity case? That I'm incapable of taking care of myself? You clearly don't know me."

"Ah, Janet. I know you as well as you know yourself. Whether that means I know you a lot or a little is tricky to say. What I can say is that you can only take care of yourself by accepting help from others. Expand your sense of oneness to the universe, and let the universe provide."

"That made absolutely no sense at all. Get out of my way, you flying freak."

"You are hasty! So are the wolves. If you don't heed my reasoning, at least consider theirs?"

Janet begrudgingly stopped walking. A howl blew from within the forest in front of her. Another sounded from her left. A third came from the forest to her right. A chorus of howls dotted the forest all around her. She was surrounded.

"You know, you really should be taking a shower," the finch said. Janet did not reply but sprinted as fast as she could back to the cabin.

CHAPTER THIRTEEN

There was no telling how long Charlando walked. He had no sense of time and could only sometimes make out the tops of buildings over the giant people all around him. However far it was, it was far enough. His legs ached, and the crowd around him was getting too handsy for his liking.

The crowd had formed one by one, as seemingly everyone who noticed Charlando had an unshakable desire to follow him. The first people to join were friendly and respectful, but as his admirers grew, so did a poisonous possessiveness amongst them. Though they all bore Charlando good intentions, they were suspicious of each other and bickered amongst themselves. An impenetrable wall of these people encircled Charlando and moved along with him as he walked. They kept a polite distance apart from him, but it was still an unnerving experience.

A loud noise in the sky stole Charlando's attention. A helicopter floated above him at the height of the buildings. It was a strange looking spaceship, he thought. The side said 'Channel 6 News'. The roar of the blades was obnoxious from a great distance away. It must have been terrible inside the craft. His own spaceship was quiet and peaceful. How lovely it would be to be there now, he thought. The crowd on the street seemed even more unsettling after thinking about his ship.

Sirens blared from down the road. They grew louder and louder until stopping a short distance away. Shouting replaced the sirens. It was not clear exactly what was happening, but it was sure that a great commotion was stirring. The noises were angry and escalating. More sirens came from down the street. Pops and bangs accompanied clouds of smoke that billowed high enough over the tops of heads for Charlando to see. The drone of the helicopter kept booming above.

The noises grew and grew and the crowd around him shook and swayed along with it. Whereas before the circle of people walked along to the pace of Charlando, it was now the circle of people that was directing Charlando's pace and direction. It bumped him along to and fro, tightening its radius as it did. Before long, the people around him were no longer at a polite distance away, but an uncomfortably close lack of a distance away.

The terror that befell Charlando was beyond any he imagined possible. The crowd would keep constricting until he was squeezed into nothingness. It was not even two days ago that he worried he was alone in the world, and here he was surrounded by so many people it would kill him. Could he have been a bigger fool?

The crowd pushed him to the edge of the sidewalk next to the building. He held his back to the glass wall and looked up at the people around him. They were all trying desperately to hold the rest of the crowd back.

A new onslaught of bangs and clouds of smoke pushed them once more. The few people protecting Charlando could not hold on any longer. They slipped and fell towards him. Charlando fell back as well, into the building. The glass behind him was a door.

Charlando's squishy butt cushioned his landing. Big Bob slammed the door shut before anyone else could come in and closed the blinds before turning on Charlando. "I told you to never come back here," he bellowed. He turned back around to peek through the blinds at the scene outside. "Did you bring your fool today?" he asked sternly.

Charlando was still spooked from his brush with death and fumbled for a coherent response. "I'm sorry, Mr. Bob. I am the only fool I know."

Bob softened at the quiver in Charlando's voice. "Are you alright boy? Did they hurt you, now?"

"I am okay. I thought I was going to be trapped there forever. Thank you for saving me."

"I did no such thing," Big Bob replied. "Those pansies out there couldn't keep water in the sea. You'd have taken them out easily enough." He bent down and effortlessly lifted Charlando back to his feet. "Now, you take a seat while I fix you a sandwich."

Charlando did as he was told and sat at the chair closest to the counter where Bob worked. The magic in Bob's hands was no less inspiring at second sight. He wanted to ask how Bob moved so beautifully, but he didn't want to interrupt his concentration. Besides, the crease of Bob's brow and cross of his eyes suggested he would not even notice Charlando's question. In that moment, Bob's world consisted solely of deli meat and accouterments.

Bob laid the finished sandwich in front of Charlando. If it weren't for the wrapping, Charlando would have devoured it before it left Bob's hands. "How do you do that?" Charlando asked.

"Do what?"

"How do you make a sandwich like that? It's the most amazing thing I've ever seen anyone do."

"That's very kind of you to say, but it sounds like you haven't seen much of the world. I'd say the way you caused that riot was a bit more peculiar."

Charlando looked back to the door. The curtains hid the outside from view, but the muffled noises coming through let him know the scene was still raging. "You think I did all that?" Charlando asked.

"Of course you did. I'm not saying you did it on purpose, but that mob didn't come from nothing. People follow you, boy. That pampered pickle you brought here last time followed you, and so did those folks on the street. Some people have that effect. I'm not one of those people. I'm not one of those pickles, either. My kindness comes free, but respect is hard earned. Now eat that sandwich."

Charlando didn't hesitate to obey. He started neatly unwrapping the sandwich, but as soon as the uncovered smell hit his nose, he stuffed his mouth with sandwich and paper alike. His tray was clear in a matter of moments. "Your kindness tastes delicious, Mr. Bob. Thank you again."

"I'm glad you can enjoy it. I might not think of you as a deity like those weenies on the street, but I can see you're a good guy. I like to know it's someone good eating my sandwiches. It makes me feel good too."

"Is that why you make sandwiches?" Charlando asked.

Big Bob stared deeply at Charlando, seemingly deciding if he was trustworthy enough for the answer. After a minute of concentration, his expression softened. "Not exactly," He began. "I do like feeding good people, but not enough to feed those rats along with them. I make sandwiches because it's the only thing I can think of that will bring me back my Beatrice." He stopped talking and looked longingly into the distance.

"Who's Beatrice? Whoever she is, I bet she would love your sandwiches."

"She didn't the last time I saw her. Maybe now it would be different. Beatrice was my wife. Still is as far as I know, but I don't know much. We were just kids when we married. I never met anyone like her. Strong as horseradish and tender as corned beef. The war had just started. It wasn't like how it is now, where nobody even thinks about it. People cared, and people believed."

"War?" Charlando questioned. "Is that what's going on outside?"

"This is exactly what I'm talking about, boy. No! I'm not talking about that hullabaloo you started. I'm talking about the real war. The one just beyond our borders. The one that's keeping them out and us in. The endless war. Let me tell you, it might be endless, but it had a beginning, and I was there. They told us we were fighting for our freedom. I know the real reason. It's The Overlords. They back both sides, trying to get the common folk to fight each other and leave the higher ups alone to do what they will. Best guess I heard was that they like to dress up as turkeys and fondle each other's snoods and wattles. They're a bunch of beastious bullies, is what they are."

Big Bob stared ahead sternly. Charlando had never heard of the war. It must be truly terrible to be worse than the terror outside. Did Beatrice also go to war? And what did this have to do with sandwiches? Big Bob seemed satisfied with what he said, but it didn't really answer the question. "Mr. Bob, what happened to Beatrice?" Charlando finally asked.

"Beatrice? That's right. I was talking about Beatrice. She was the most beautiful girl I ever met. Her skin was as smooth as a tomato.

She was classy as an olive, too. Boy, thinking of her is like cutting an onion." Big Bob sniffled and dabbed his eyes with a handkerchief he pulled out of his pocket.

"She sounds perfect. I'm terribly sorry you lost her. Did she go to war too?"

"Beatrice go to war? Not a chance. She saw what it was right away. She begged me not to go, but I had to. A man my age didn't really have a choice. I made sure we were married before I left, though. You don't let a girl like Beatrice stay single. She said she would wait for me. We were so in love, I believed her. Never would have gone if I thought it meant losing her."

"She left you while you went to war? That's awful!"

"No, no boy. She waited for me. I wasn't gone long. There was an accident. Well, I can't in good conscience call it an accident. I was a chicken. I've never been much for fighting, and when the time came, I ran so fast I fell and hit my head so hard it near' broke in two. I suppose it was my heart that took the brunt of the fall, though I didn't know it for some years to come. I was out cold for two weeks after that. They weren't sure if I was ever going to wake up again. If you ask Beatrice, she might say I never did."

"She left while you were in a coma? Big Bob, that is the most hurtful thing I've ever heard!"

"For God's sake boy, didn't I tell you she was sweet as honey mustard? She nursed me back to health, and I was no easy baby. I was full of rage and didn't know why. People called us names, but that wasn't it. I kept forgetting stuff, but Beatrice would always remind me. I still can't figure out where all that anger came from. It was like a dam broke in my head and all the anger I stored my whole life came flooding out. Beatrice may have been the only person I ever knew who didn't deserve that, and she's the one who got it. I never laid a finger on her, boy, you best be clear, but God dang-it, I did her wrong.

One day, I couldn't find my pants. I looked everywhere: the bathroom, the kitchen, tool shed. I lost control of myself. Yelling and screaming. Beatrice had just gone to the store, and I went looking for her. 'Beatrice,' I yelled. 'Where are my pants!' I ran all through town looking for her. I finally found her at the deli getting some ham. The look she gave me was one I'll never forget. There was so much fear and so much sadness. Then she blinked and it was gone. Her eyes were clear. Her expression melted from her face. 'Did you check your pants drawer?' she asked so quiet' I could barely hear. I couldn't believe I hadn't thought of it. 'No, mam,' I whispered back. Then she walked away, and I never saw her again. I figured she was at that deli because she wanted a ham sandwich. It's hard not to think that I'll never see her again, but if I do, I will make the best ham sandwich she's ever had."

This information was startling to Charlando. Big Bob had been in love with a woman who loved him, and he drove her away. Love is kind and warm and full of joy. Yet Mr. Bob is miserable. In all his lessons about love, he never once heard anything that suggested such an outcome was possible. Could Bob and Beatrice really have been in love?

"Mr. Bob," Charlando began, "were you and Beatrice in love? Most of your story sounds like it, but the ending most certainly did not. Now that I think about it, I never thought there was an ending to love."

"Were we in love? I know I was. Still am." Bob wiped a tear from his eye and composed himself. "My fear is that she never loved me back. I think maybe she could feel me loving her, and we were both just confused about the source of that feeling. I watch the pickles that come in to get my sandwiches, and that's what I see in them.

One guy or girl will have a sphere of light around them. It glows bright as the full moon. Then some flickering firefly will cozy up next to them. You have to pay attention to see the light's not coming from both of them. I suppose we were both in love. It was just my love, and when she left, all that love stayed with me."

Big Bob stopped talking and stared ahead to the closed door, maybe wondering if Beatrice would ever walk through. Charlando looked at his sadness and wondered about what he said. The spaceship's computer never talked about love this way, or at least Charlando never paid attention while it did. The way Bob talked about it, love was a curse. Love was a bubble in which he was trapped, and Beatrice used to shelter momentarily before skipping away. Is that what Janet did to him?

A loud rattle distracted them both and directed their attention to a vent above them. It shook and banged. One of the anchors holding it to the ceiling snapped, and then another. The vent split open and a tall, strong, handsome man plummeted down to the table in front of Charlando.

CHAPTER FOURTEEN

Alexander somersaulted out of the vent and landed cat-like in a crouched position, ready to pounce. An alien-sized bag clasped tight in his hand. He was face to face with the slimy green object of his mission. The helpless alien was stunned speechless, and the fat man in the soiled apron screamed and hid behind the counter. Destiny stared him straight in the face. At last, Alexander Machomole would be the hero he was always meant to be: The Savior of the Universe.

He inhaled the sweet smell of triumph. It was like no smell he had ever smelled. Not sweet at all, in fact, but briny and pungent. It was actually quite foul. Was this why Freddy always looked like he was smelling a fart? No, this was something different, and foul though it was, it was far from repulsive. It tugged on something buried deep within him, drawing out a part of himself that had only ever faced inward.

The bag in Alexander's hand slipped out. There was nothing traditionally appealing about the alien's appearance. His face was like one giant blemish. His body was more of an onion-shape than hourglass or triangle. The little hair he had on his head was greasy and as thick as toothpicks. Yet somewhere in Charlando's disgusting skin folds, Alexander fumbled his affection. This was the most beautiful creature he had ever seen.

The slimy, green creature before him blinked back into motion and swallowed away his speechlessness. "You gave me quite a fright, sir," He squeaked. "My name is Charlando, and that's Mr. Bob hiding behind the counter."

"You best leave us alone, you flabbering fatty," Bob yelped from behind the counter. "I'll stick you with this salami. I swear to you I will!" Bob was completely hidden, but a giant stick of salami flopped in the air above the counter like a friendly sock puppet.

"I mean you no harm," Alexander said, with just a little less of his usual gusto. "I came to capture, or save rather, your friend. Charlando, it is a pleasure to meet you. My name is Alexander Machomole."

"You think you can break into my shop and steal my friend? You're a dirty son of a dandy and you ain't going nowhere with that boy," Bob shouted back, now standing to his full height and waving the salami at Alexander.

As big as Big Bob was, it was mostly in circumference. He was not the least bit intimidating to the heavily armed, incomparably trained, secret agent who considered himself the savior of the universe. Alexander too stood to his full height. From atop the table, his head grazed the exposed pipes on the ceiling. "I said my name is Alexander Machomole," he began, his confidence fully restored. "If that name means nothing to you, then you mean nothing to this world. I've saved your planet more times than you've played with those sausages, and now I'm here to save Charlando." He posed with his hands triumphantly at his hips to allow his words to sink in.

Charlando applauded from behind him, clearly impressed by the entrance. "It's so wonderful to meet you, Mr. Machomole! I'm grateful for the gesture, but Mr. Bob here already saved me. He even made me a sandwich. They're the best around, if you can believe it. Hey, Mr. Bob! Why not make our new friend a sandwich too?"

"I ain't making that hunk of ham nothing," Bob grumbled back.

"I didn't come here to save you from that little parade outside," Alexander began, "and I certainly didn't come for a sad sack's sandwich." He turned briefly to Bob who sank at his intimidating gaze. "You are in more danger than you realize, and I'm the only one who can help you."

"More danger than all of that?" Charlando looked back to the door and trembled. The pops and bangs and yells and screams had only gotten louder.

"You're being tracked by the government. They mean to capture you before anyone else finds out you exist."

"Capture me?" Charlando asked. "Why would they want to do that?"

"I suspect it's for science. If I know anything about scientists, they will strip you down and probe every hole they can find."

Bob shot up from behind the counter once again. "I told you they were beastious bullies," he yelled before deflating from Alexander's renewed stare.

Alexander turned back to see Charlando sink into his chair. All the giddiness he showed moments before was gone. His face was discomforting to see, not because of its grossly misshapen form, but because it was so full of sadness. It was true that he was in danger of being probed, and that Alexander must protect him from that grizzly end, but there was apparently more from which he needed protection. Charlando was so weak and gentle, even knowing of the possibility of being probed was too much for him to handle. He needed protection from the truth.

"Don't be afraid," Alexander said. "No one can harm you while I'm around."

Charlando looked up and smiled feebly. "Thank you, sir. I don't mean to be gloomy. I just don't understand how a world full of friendly people can be so dangerous. Everyone I've met has been kind to me and terribly untrusting of everyone else. How can that be?"

Alexander pondered this question for a moment while hopping off the table. What could he say to satisfy Charlando's curiosity without jeopardizing his sense of safety? The truth was that although most people are genuinely kindhearted, there are a great many who are not, and it is very difficult to tell them apart. Some, like Freddy, are brutally sadistic. Even if there were just one such person out of every hundred, it stands to reason that you should be very careful of who is around you; there is always one nearby. But the truth is even scarier. There are people, like Freddy, who are not just brutally sadistic, but also highly ambitious and gifted. These are the people who keep the whole world on edge.

"They are just dumb," Alexander finally said. "There is no need to worry."

"He's lying to you, boy!" Bob yelled from behind the counter.

"This is exactly what I'm talking about," Alexander said, pointing to the counter. "That is a kind man over there. Kind and dumb. He hides like a child because he is dumb like a child. Does that make sense, Charlando?"

"I suppose so. I don't totally understand, but I don't seem to understand most things these days."

"Don't trust him, boy!" Bob said from behind the counter, though it looked like the salami sock puppet was the one talking. Alexander took two steps to the counter and yanked it away. Bob gave one last fearful yelp and then stayed quiet.

"I couldn't help but overhear you talking about love," Alexander began. "I didn't mean to intrude on a private conversation, but I also couldn't help but be concerned. You shouldn't get any ideas about women from Little Bob here. If you want to get a woman to like you, you need to listen to someone who's successful with women."

There was a whimper from behind the counter, but no other response.

"Where do I find someone like that?" Charlando asked.

"Well, I'm not one to pay myself compliments," Alexander said nonchalantly while looking at his nails, "but, someone like that just found you." He looked up to Charlando, expecting more enthusiasm from the confused Ooflan. "Me, Charlando. I am successful with women, and I can help you get Janet."

"You really mean it?" Charlando gasped. An air of suspicion still clung to him.

"Of course I am successful with women. I am Alexander Machomole. I'd tell you how much success I've had, but I don't want to make your sad friend even sadder. You give me one day, and I'll give you a whole life with that girl."

Charlando took no further convincing. He shot up from his chair and hugged Alexander's leg. "Thank you, thank you," he shouted. "You really did come here to save me. I was beginning to worry that I would be alone forever."

"Lesson number one," Alexander said, "don't worry about anything. That's a woman's job. If you do the woman's job for her, why would she stick around?"

Bob stirred from his submission. "Don't listen to that nonsense! He's poisoning your mind, boy!"

Alexander waved off the interruption. Bob's opinion was as meaningful as a dog's. "It's up to you. If you don't want my help, then tell me now. You can hide behind that counter with your friend and drown your sorrows in mayonnaise."

Charlando's slimy face scrunched tight with consideration. He shook a little while he thought. "I would like your help, Mr. Machomole," he said after some time. "I'm sorry, Mr. Bob. I know you don't trust him, but if I want to find Janet and make her love me, I have to take a chance. I won't find her here eating sandwiches. And when I do find her, I don't want to lose her. I need Mr. Machomole's help."

Bob rose slowly from behind the counter. His face ran red with tears. "I understand, boy. Truth is, I won't find Beatrice here either. A part of me thinks I make these sandwiches because I know it keeps me from finding her, because losing her again would be too painful. I'm a chicken, boy. You don't need a chicken telling you what's what. Go on. Get your Janet. Just make sure you stay true to yourself. You're a good man, and there's nothing you can be that's more valuable than that."

Charlando and Bob looked into each other's crying eyes for some time. Alexander thought this behavior would likely be repulsive to a woman, but could not adequately phrase why, so he said nothing. Though he would never admit it to anyone, he wanted to cry with them. Instead, he shoved his weakness to the side and broke up the sentimental moment. "You just let me know when you babies are done," he said before strutting towards the window. He made it look like he was checking the scene outside, but really he was hiding the single salty drip that escaped his right eye.

"Mr. Machomole," Charlando croaked after a short time, "I think I am ready now."

Alexander turned back around. He used the curtain to dry his face as he spun. "The babies are done crying, huh? Finally. Get your stuff then. We're getting out of here."

"Where are we going?" Charlando asked.

Alexander had not thought that far ahead. He did not, in fact, know anything about Janet or Charlando or how to make one like the other. The urge to help Charlando sprung up so suddenly and with such bewitchment that his promises came swifter than his mind could keep. "We're going back to my hotel," he said after a short pause. "It's across the street from yours. We'll discuss things further when we get there." He stretched out the last few words to buy as much time as he could to think of a plan.

"That's an awfully far way to walk. Would it be okay with you if we drove?"

Alexander considered the mob in the street and what it would mean to be seen helping the alien he was sent to capture. He looked at Charlando and then at the bag laying on the table next to them. "I will carry you in that bag," he said.

"The bag?" Charlando squeaked. "I suppose if that's what you think is right."

"You're getting kidnapped, boy!" Bob objected.

"Charlando made his decision, and you'll do best to respect it," Alexander responded.

Charlando and Bob exchanged sad looks once more. "If I have to be kidnapped to get to Janet, then that is what I'll do. Goodbye, Mr. Bob. You can put me in the bag now."

Charlando and Bob's eye contact broke only from the cover of fabric the Ooflan disappeared behind. Alexander drew the bag down to Charlando's feet and hoisted him up over his shoulder. Alexander held both ends of the bag so the alien hung in the sack like a hammock. "Do you have a backdoor by any chance?" Alexander asked Bob.

"No sir. An honest man has no use for one," Bob whimpered.

"Very well. I hope you're comfortable, boy. This may get rough."

Alexander turned and strutted to the front door. He slid open the blind and looked outside for an opportune time to bully through the crowd. The unruly mob showed no sign of relent. An easier way would not present itself for hours, and to wait would undermine Alexander's image of strength and authority. Bob's whimpering in the background was a reminder of the importance of that. Alexander bullishly opened the door. The wash of noise chewed away his last grip of indecision, and with one step forward, the crowd swallowed them whole.

CHAPTER FIFTEEN

Charlando swung into the air and thudded on a hard mattress, bouncing twice before coming to a rest on the springy surface. It did not have the same sleep-inducing quality of his own mattress, but all for the better at the moment. He was eager to learn the secrets of courtship from Alexander, who had shared less than expected on the walk to the hotel. It was understandable during the riot. He would not have been able to hear much over the sounds of that commotion. Alexander had lifted him high above his head to keep him from being squashed, but the shaking from people bumping into Alexander was still too mighty a distraction. No, Charlando could not expect his lessons to have begun then. But what about the long walk after? The mob was condensed around a single block. Charlando didn't hear hardly a patter beyond that. Yet, Alexander was adamant that the lesson should start at the hotel. Fortunately, waiting was something at which Charlando excelled.

Alexander pulled the bag off Charlando and tossed it to the ground. He looked weary from the journey. Carrying an Ooflan must be quite the chore. Charlando looked down at his bulging body. Of course Alexander couldn't start the lessons. If it wasn't because he was too winded from carrying him, it was because he realized there was no helping such a fat pile of slime.

"Are you feeling okay?" Alexander asked. "You were so excited on the walk over here. Why the sudden sadness?"

"I'm sorry Mr. Machomole. I'm sorry for making you carry me all that way and I'm sorry for enlisting you in such a hopeless task. Look at me, and look at you. What could I possibly learn to overcome this hideous body of mine."

"Quit whining, boy. I could carry ten of you up a mountain. You alone on flat streets is no trouble at all. And as for your appearance, it's no concern. Women don't care what you look like, unless, of course, you look like me. I admit there are advantages I was born with—my impeccable facial features, for instance—but what matters most is how you carry yourself, the attention your presence demands. In that, you are a worthy pupil. You must be strong of mind and will. Don't ever apologize for your presence, and don't ever show fear."

The ring of the phone silenced him. Alexander looked as though it were a siren catching him mid heist. "Don't make a sound," he said with a finger to his lips. The pair held their breath as the phone rang a few more times before falling silent.

"Why did that thing make you so frightened?" Charlando asked.

"Frightened? Of the phone? Don't be ridiculous, Charlando. I am never afraid." A new onslaught of rings made Alexander jump. "Good God," he said. "I will have to answer it this time. Keep quiet."

Alexander went to the phone and answered, "Alexander speaking."

A long-winded retort sputtered from the receiving end that Charlando could not understand.

"Don't worry, Mr. President. I will have the alien to you before you know it."

More nonsense spewed from the other end of the phone.

"You will do what to him?" Alexander asked. "Maybe it would be better to treat him well. Maybe get him in a jacuzzi, play some Jazz and rub his feet."

The screeches that blew from the phone were so sharp and loud that Alexander moved it two feet from his ear to continue the conversation.

"Mr. President, I assure you, I am handling it. There is no need to get Freddy involved. Such a cunning and dangerous foe demands patience and vigorous attention to detail. I just need a little more time to capture him safely. You can desecrate his body however you'd like after that… Yes, that would be a wonderful way to disembowel an alien… Very well… Thank you Mr. President... Bye-bye now."

Alexander hung up the phone and rolled onto the bed. He lay flat on his back with his hands covering his face. If he weren't incapable of weakness, Charlando would say he looked utterly defeated. "Was that a friend of yours?" Charlando asked.

"You're the only friend I have left, green man. My only concern now is for your safety." Alexander paused and looked around at his hotel room. Charlando looked around too. The stains on the curtains tinted the light coming through the windows, so the whole room glowed a musky yellow. The wallpaper cracked and peeled and was splotched with the remnants of mystery liquids that splattered and dripped to the bottom. The bed beneath them was as stiff as the floor. The sheets on top were the consistency of construction paper. The only highlight of the room was how little of it there was to be disgusted by.

"You know, Charlando," Alexander began, "I think we would be better off in your suite at the Marvaloo. Women always prefer luxury. They might not say it outright, but reality speaks for itself. What do you think?"

"That sounds like a great idea!" Charlando said. "Your room is nice, but I like the way my suite does not remind me of poo."

"That is indeed a good quality. I of course would also be staying there, but my job demands that I keep a low profile. I will make an exception on your behalf."

"Thank you, sir. And what do you do for work? I feel so selfish for having not asked before!"

"What do I do for work?" Alexander repeated. "Well, I protect people. I suppose some might call me a hero."

"I should have known that's what you were! Mother told me all about heroes. How they are brave and selfless and sacrifice themselves for the good of others. But it all makes sense now! Oh, how splendid I feel to have you, a real hero at my service. And this must mean what Mother said about love was true too! Janet really is my soulmate and I hers, and you will help me find her! Thank you, Mr. Machomole! Thank you!" Charlando, overcome with giddiness, rolled on the hard bed, flipping backwards all the way to his feet. "Let us go, great hero!"

The rousing speech brought Alexander to attention. He stood tall and strong as the heroes of Mother's stories. "We will find your Janet, no matter the odds. I don't care how many agents of death are hunting you down. If they want to slice you open, they will have to go through me."

"Agents of death?" Charlando muttered. That part did not sound like anything in Mother's story.

"Forget I said that. It's a figure of speech. Now let's leave before Freddy gets here."

Alexander lifted Charlando off the bed before he could ask any more questions. Charlando took a moment to steady himself, and they both headed out the door and down the hall. Alexander sped well ahead before realizing the slowness of Charlando's wobbly gait. "Is that the fastest you walk?" Alexander asked.

Charlando, already panting from the exertion, leaned on the wall for support. "I am not sure if it is the fastest I can go, but it is the fastest I have ever gone. Would it be alright if we took a little break?"

"A break? We haven't even made it down the hall. You're telling me you can't walk down the hall without needing a break, and you wonder why that girl doesn't like you?"

Charlando gasped. He looked back at how far they came. The short distance brought him shame. What could he offer Janet, the most beautiful girl in the world, if he could not walk a few feet without succumbing to exhaustion? "I do not wonder why she doesn't like me, but what I can do to change it. I see everyone else walking fast and easy with their long legs and skinny bodies, and I know I can't compete. What can I do?"

"You can start by sucking it up and being a man. No one likes a complainer. Second, you need new shoes. You're an attractive guy, but no respectable woman would be with a man who wears those shoes."

"I never thought about my shoes before," Charlando said. He looked down towards his feet, but all he saw was his bulging belly. "Am I wearing shoes?"

"I can't tell," Alexander said slowly. He bent over to get a better look. "You better hope Janet doesn't have a thing for feet. Where did you meet her anyways?"

"Oh Alexander, it was the most magical occasion. I was walking in the park under a star filled sky. Nobody else was around, and I couldn't bear to take another step for the loneliness I felt was too much. I wished as hard as I could for the universe to send me the love of my life so I wouldn't have to feel such an awful feeling anymore. And wouldn't you know it? I heard Janet screaming from just down the path. Can you believe I found her asleep on a bench at 4:00 in the morning?"

Alexander groaned and pressed his hand to his forehead. "You've never been with a girl, have you?"

"Well, that's the most miraculous part. She's the first person I ever met! Can you believe my luck?" Charlando smiled broadly.

Alexander shook his head with his mouth hung slack. "Kid, there aren't many respectable women found on park benches at four in the morning. I'm not saying anything bad about her, but, well, you might stand a better chance with her than you think. You might not even need new shoes."

"You really mean it?" Charlando asked.

"She sounds desperate. I think all you need is a bed, and she's yours, but you should slow down. If you really like this girl, you should get the new shoes anyways. You have to look like you have other options, even if you don't want them, otherwise she'll just walk all over you."

"Even if she's kind and true?" Charlando asked. "Janet is a special lady, you know."

"Yeah, yeah. They say no two snowflakes are alike, but I've seen a million, and they all look the same to me. If you're not taking care of yourself, she's going to walk all over you."

"If that's what makes her happy, then she can walk on me as much as she likes."

"That won't make her happy. If you want her to be happy, you need new shoes."

"You sure do know a lot about women."

Alexander kneeled to eye-level. His strong hands fell on Charlando's ambiguous shoulders. "I will teach you what I can, but right now we need to leave. I will carry you the rest of the way." Alexander swept Charlando off his feet and cradled him like a baby. They hurried together down the hall to the elevator.

"Will you teach me to be as strong as you are?" Charlando asked.

"No one can be as strong as I am. I will teach you how to dress yourself so you don't look like a turd rolled in trash."

"Oh, thank you! Thank you!"

The elevator door closed and the two fell to the lobby. Alexander did not spare a needless moment in the hotel. He rushed out and across the empty street to the Chateau Marvaloo. Danny still stood outside ready to welcome them.

"Charlando! It's so wonderful to have you back. Some of the guys thought you were leaving for good, but I knew better. And you brought a friend! Good afternoon, sir. My name is Danny. Would you like any help carrying your things?" Danny looked politely around for luggage.

"You do not need to know my name," Alexander responded stiffly. "And Charlando is not luggage. We will be going to his room alone."

"Of course, sir. I wish you a pleasant day," Danny said as Alexander bullied past.

"It was good to see you too, Danny! Sorry about Alexander!" Charlando shouted while being carried through the hotel's revolving doors.

Just one of the girls stood behind the reception desk this time of day. Otherwise, the lobby was empty. Without obstruction from busy bodies, the echoes of trickling fountains reverberated around the marbled room. The resonance was enchanting. Alexander softened his steps to match its timbre but kept a swift pace to the lone girl.

The girl kept her doe like eyes steadied upon them as they approached. "Good afternoon, gentlemen. How can I help you?" she said soft and clear.

"We need a key to Charlando's room," Alexander said.

"I can absolutely do that for you. Do you have any identification I can use to verify the reservation?"

Alexander hoisted Charlando towards her. Charlando smiled and waved at the young woman who grimaced before righting herself.

"Ahh, of course. Here is a key to the room, and here is this as well," She said, handing Charlando the key and an envelope with 'Charlando' written in fancy cursive. "It is from Mr. Hinkle. He said he was very sorry for what happened earlier and wanted to give you this to hopefully begin to make up for it."

Charlando took it slowly from the receptionist. "Thank you," he said, taking in the gift. "You can tell Mr. Hinkle that I don't know what this paper means, but it won't make me forget how he behaved this morning. And though I have come back, I did not do so to see him."

"I will let him know," she said politely. A longing smile replaced the grimace on her face.

"We have to get going now. Thanks for the key, miss," Alexander said with a wink.

The receptionist made a dirty look at him before smiling once again at Charlando. "Farewell, Charlando," she said sweetly. "If you need anything at all, you just have to ask."

"Thank you, Mrs. Key Lady. I will keep that in mind."

Alexander pulled Charlando back into his cradling arms and turned. They walked to the elevator at the end of the lobby. The lullaby of fountains once again encompassed them. Charlando's eyes grew heavy, and a yawn escaped him. Sleep was about to take hold, but the ping of the elevator broke the enchantment. Alexander carried him inside and pushed a button in the tree of lights next to the door. "That girl was all over you, boy. If things don't work out with Janet, you should give her a call."

"What are you talking about?"

"That receptionist wants you, Charlando. Did you not notice? Surely you think she's attractive."

"Well, yes. I thought she was beautiful. She was so beautiful in fact that I had trouble forming words when at first she looked at me, but then I thought of Janet. I do not believe I could love another. You know, when I was coming to this planet, I saw more stars than I could possibly count. More than I can believe exist even after seeing them myself. But once I got close to the sun, I haven't been able to see any others. That one star shines so brightly in my eyes that a sky full of other stars—an infinite number of them, and many bigger and brighter than the sun—is completely invisible in its presence. And even when the sun is lost from the sky, the moon still beams its reflection brighter than the rest of stars combined. When I met Janet, I saw the sun, and I will never see another in the same way again."

The elevator pinged and the doors opened. Alexander was slow to leave and had to raise his arm to block the doors from sliding shut again. "You're a remarkable man," he said. "You have not been on this planet long enough to realize how special you are, but in time I think the whole world will know. Janet amongst them." He gently set Charlando to his feet and looked up, gasping at what he saw.

The hallway to Charlando's room was dressed floor to ceiling in strings of balloons and streamers of ribbons and flowers. The way was lined with cart after cart of food. It was every offering the hotel's kitchen could imagine, from towering cake to dripping roasts of ham. Above the door to the master suite was a message in big sparkling letters: 'Please forgive me'.

"What the heck did that man do to you?" Alexander asked.

The smell of ham made it difficult to remember what it was that Mr. Hinkle did wrong. "I think he said something about Janet," he mumbled in a trance. Was this such a great wrong that he must reject his offering of ham?

"Interesting. I'll be sure not to do the same."

"Thank you, and could you put that tray on the ground for me as well?" Charlando asked, pointing at a steaming ham.

Alexander looked curiously at the ham and shrugged. "Of course. Are you hungry?" he asked while setting the tray down.

Charlando did not answer the question. Instead, he flopped to the floor and ravaged the ham. Bits and pieces of ham flew around him like grass clippings from a weed whacker. In the storm of ham bits, Mr. Hinkle's letter flew out too.

Alexander noticed the letter and picked it up. "Do you mind if I open this, Charlando?" Alexander asked.

The pool of ham drippings on the platter was too engrossing for Charlando to reply. He slurped up the last lapping of savory ham syrup and collapsed on his back next to the now sparkling clean plate. Alexander stood above him reading the letter, having taken his moans of pleasure as an affirmative response to his question.

"This can't be," Alexander said to himself.

"What is that Mr. Machomole?" Charlando burped.

"It's another reason to be mad at Mr. Hinkle. Maybe the biggest yet."

"Oh no! And to think I was just about ready to forgive him. What did he do this time?"

"It's a thoughtful gesture, no doubt. Unfortunately, it's the thought of a very stupid man. He's throwing you a party tomorrow night here at The Marvaloo. He says he's releasing a public statement asking Janet to come. He's also posting these fliers all over town."

Alexander handed a piece of paper to Charlando. Its content eluded the illiterate Ooflan, but the presentation captivated him. The pretty colors and wavy lines were delightful. "A party for me and Janet? But that sounds wonderful! Oh, this is just what I needed. If Janet sees this message, she'll be sure to come!"

"She's not the only one," Alexander replied.

"What's that supposed to mean?" Charlando asked. "Oh, I don't care so long as Janet is there. You will help me get ready, won't you? I wouldn't want her to see me like this." Charlando moved his hands across his greasy body. He still lay on the floor surrounded by ham bits.

"You look as handsome as ever, Charlando, and I will, of course, help you get ready. If this hallway is any indication, that party will be a spectacle of decadence and love enough to fill your mind with nothing but joy. No fear should taint that sacred space. What uninvited danger attends is for me to guess and bear alone."

CHAPTER SIXTEEN

Janet laid curled on the couch for hours in the same pink pajamas soaking up the stink of her unshowered body and suspicious mind. The clean set of Merideth's clothes sat on the table before her. To use her shower and wear her clothes was to ignore betrayal and become further indebted to a treacherous foe. Merideth presented herself so sweetly to Janet's face, but she stabbed her back the moment it turned. What disparaging tales was she telling the rest of the commune now? She knew about her drinking. Does she know about her parents too? Has her coffer of secrets spilled so completely?

A knock on the door startled her. "Hey Janet," Merideth said, "Is it alright if I come in?

Janet stayed glued to the couch. She had sunk into her mind so deeply it took another round of knocking for the connection to her body to return to her. Her muscles throbbed awake all at once and she sprung to her feet.

Merideth looked frightened when Janet swung open the door. Her balled fist hung in the air ready to knock once more. "Hello," she said. "How's your day going? I thought you might be taking a nap or something, so I didn't come sooner. Oh, you didn't take a shower. That's fine. You can always take one later."

Janet stared silently. Her bitter inner voice didn't make it to her lips.

"Well," Meredith continued, "I just came by to let you know we're starting the meeting soon. I don't think I can handle those idiots by myself anymore. That probably doesn't make you want to go, but I would really love it if you did."

Janet remained silent. It would be suspicious if she didn't go to the meeting. As far as they knew, that is the only reason she came. If she wasn't there, they would ask questions and Meredith would be the one to answer them in any way she wanted.

"I can tell them you're not feeling well if you want," Merideth offered.

"No. I will go."

"That's great! Did you need to get ready at all?" Merideth asked, looking down at Janet's pajamas.

"I'm ready now, thank you."

"Ok," Merideth said feebly.

They walked together across the commune, a collection of eight cabins similar to Richard's and Merideth's surrounding a large vegetable garden. "This used to be a health retreat," Merideth said as they walked. "Richard's dad bought it and closed it down. He owns a chain of fast-food restaurants and didn't want anyone in town to come here and learn about vegetables. He'd probably disown

Richard if he ever found out what he was using this place for. Luckily he doesn't care enough about him to pay attention."

Something about walking and listening to someone else's story softened Janet's suspicious thoughts and freed her curiosity. "What does Richard tell his dad he does?" she asked.

Merideth lit up at the first glint of cheerfulness Janet showed. "He just tells him he's into publication. His dad assumes he's climbing the ranks of some big newspaper or publishing house. Richard doesn't like to lie and he doesn't even have to with him. He says that's the good part about selfish people. You can tell them the truth without worrying they'll listen or ask questions."

They stopped at a cabin at the end of the garden. "This is it," Merideth said, turning to face Janet. "You haven't met anyone but me and Richard, have you?"

Janet shook her head no.

"Just remember, they're weird, but they aren't dangerous, and you can always go back to our cabin if you want."

"I think I prefer weird people," Janet said.

"Then you've come to the right place," Merideth replied. She smiled and hopped up the stairs to the front door, giving one last excited look before pushing it open and ushering Janet in like an honored guest.

Janet was met with boisterous greetings from a group of six young men circled around Richard who held a guitar by the fireplace. The cabin was laid out just like Merideth's, except that the bedroom wall was knocked out, creating one giant room with a kitchen and bathroom. Two more men poked their heads out of the kitchen and raised their beers in acknowledgment of the new guest. One older man sat in a recliner on the far end of the room and did not take any notice of Janet at all. He stared straight ahead at a small tv tuned to the local news. His head was wrapped in tin foil and a cigarette burned in his hand hovering over an overflowing ashtray.

"Janet! You made it!" Richard said excitedly. He set down his guitar and stood up. "Guys, this is Janet. She's here to help with the paper."

The six men on the couch and two in the kitchen said 'Hi Janet' like a bunch of nervous schoolboys.

"They don't see many girls around here," Meredith whispered to Janet. Janet did not see many boys either, and would have been much more intimidated if it weren't for the group of men's utter lack of masculinity. She smiled and waved at them feeling, if anything, a touch more power than she had before.

"Hey, make some room for them, guys," Richard said to the group.

"Of course!" One the boys on the couch closer to the door croaked. He jumped up and squeezed on to the other couch. The two boys remaining saw what he did and leapt up to do the same. There was now one couch with six boys packed like sardines and another empty for the girls to sit.

"I told you they were weird and harmless," Meredith whispered to Janet and then laughed loud enough for everyone to hear. The two girls made their way to their couch and sat down.

"This is Jareth, Jorkin, Jasper, Donald, Deedris and Diddle," Richard said, pointing to each boy on the couch. "And that's Humphry and Hubert in the kitchen. Casper's on the chair in the back, but he usually just sticks to himself."

"It's nice to meet you all," Janet said politely.

"It's nice to meet you, too," piped Jareth.

"I'm so glad you came," croaked Deedris.

"You're very pretty," said Humphry, who blushed and disappeared nervously into the kitchen. The rest stayed quiet and stiff.

"Well, alright," Richard said enthusiastically. "Let's get started. I believe last week we decided to focus on the war again. Did anyone do any research this week?" The boys were silent. Their eyes were wide and fearful. They tried to hide behind one another, but because they were all trying this at the same time, they ended up just squeezing even closer together. "Well, try again next week," Richard continued. "Merideth, do you want to fill us in on what's been happening?"

"Yes," Merideth said, her smile fading at once. "The government's propaganda machine is telling us they're winning the fight and need a surge of recruits to finish the job quickly." The way her voice commanded the room took Janet off guard. The boys on the couch unclenched from each other and stared slack jawed at Merideth. Even Humphry peaked his head around the doorway to listen. "But my sources suggest otherwise. The front is being pushed towards us. Johnstown, just 80 miles to the south, is now being bombed on the daily. It's just a matter of time before we get hit here too. They're afraid if people find out about their incompetence in the war, it will provoke revolution. I say we test that theory."

The news shook the room. "Johnstown? My grandma lives there," Jorkin piped up.

"I hope grandma has a bomb shelter," Merideth replied. "She'll need it." Jorkin's beady eyes darted around the room, and he whimpered. "The time for playing frisbee at the park has come to an end. We must act now and with force. If we break into the Channel 6 news station, we can send a live report from Gurgleburg to Stinkton. The truth must be heard. Now, who's with me?"

Uneasy murmurings filled the room. Even the ever-jovial Richard looked too troubled to speak. Merideth rose from her seat, silencing the frightened group of boys. Her command of the room was almost completely unopposed. There was just one set of eyes that did not cower.

Casper, still staring straight at the television, guffawed loud enough for everyone to turn. "The real war is just getting started. That petty squabble you're talking about won't mean nothing when the real war comes, and Channel 6 has been covering it all day."

"What are you talking about?" Merideth asked, exacerbated.

"See for yourself, girl," Casper said, pointing at the screen. Everyone in the room gathered around the television to see. It was repeating footage of a riot earlier in the day with the caption 'Green Man Cult Clashes with Police'. "I've been waiting for this day all my life. That's an alien, girl, and as soon as the government gets hold of it, the rest will come looking. That's when the real war starts. You want to be a hero, you best save that little green fella."

"This is ridiculous," Merideth said. "There is an actual war 80 miles to the south of here, and the news station is reporting about some stupid alien conspiracy. We have to act now."

Richard did not seem to be listening to Merideth and instead sat in front of the television and turned up the volume. "The cult leader has yet to be identified," the newsman said, "but police have released this image of the man. They ask that anyone with information of his name or whereabouts call this hotline immediately."

A blurry close-up of a slimy green creature flashed on the screen, along with a number for the hotline. It looked familiar to Janet. She could not remember where she had seen him before, but she did feel a sudden craving for a sandwich.

Richard stood up and turned to the rest of the room. "Casper is right," he said. "We need to protect that beautiful creature."

"Did you just call that thing beautiful?" Merideth asked.

"I did because he is. I saw him yesterday in that exact same spot. He was going into Big Bob's Sandwich Shop, and I couldn't help but wait to see him leave. I don't know what happened, but Big Bob chased him off. He was with some other man who looked suspicious. It must have been him that Bob didn't like. Anyways, I've been thinking about him ever since. I didn't want to bring him up because I didn't think you guys would believe me, but that was wrong of me. He is real, and we need to save him!"

The rest of the group, aside from Casper and the girls, nodded excitedly to each other. It was clear that they much preferred the idea of finding a friendly alien to hijacking a news station. Merideth was not as easily convinced. "We need to stop this war. No one will be safe when planes are bombing every corner of the city. We don't know where to find that thing anyways. The police can't even find him!"

Richard didn't respond, seeming to realize his powerlessness in the situation. He turned around sullenly to listen to the news anchor. "And this just in, we have found a man claiming to know the green man personally. We go live now to the Chateau Marvaloo. Marvin?"

"That's right, Al," a different reporter chimed in. "I am standing here with Mr. Hinkle, the general manager at the Chateau Marvaloo. Mr. Hinkle, you claim to know the green man personally do you not?"

"I most certainly do, Marvin," Mr. Hinkle said, yanking the microphone from Marvin's hand. "Like all important people, he is staying right here at The Marvaloo, and if you're listening right now, Charlando, I want to say that I hope you enjoyed your ham. If you need any more, or anything else, you just let anyone at the hotel know. We will bring you as many hams as you would like." He paused briefly to beat away Marvin who tried reaching for the microphone.

"I would also like to take this time to announce that there will be a party tomorrow night here at the Marvaloo for Charlando and his beloved Janet. Janet, wherever you are, please come to The Chateau Marvaloo tomorrow night at 7. You and Charlando will be honored together with the most spectacular entertainment and copious libations this town has ever seen. Thank you." Mr. Hinkle slammed the microphone back in Marvin's chest.

Richard swung back around to Janet. "He's not talking about you, is he?"

"I don't know," Janet said slowly, thinking hard about why the green man looked so familiar. The memory of Charlando was slow to creep back into Janet's mind. She was too drunk to remember most nights, and the night she met Charlando was particularly hazy. She remembered going home to write that night and deciding to clean. And then she remembered waking up on a bench the next morning smelling like smoke. She also remembered waking up with a strange dream about a creature who reminded her of her father. That creature said he was going to bring her a sandwich. Could that have been more than a dream?

"I remember meeting someone small and green, but I thought it was just my imagination," she said at last.

"So it is you!" Richard said triumphantly before falling to one knee. "Janet, forgive me if I have done anything to dishonor you. It would be my greatest pleasure to take you to that party tomorrow night and deliver you to the Green Man."

"Are you guys kidding me right now?" Merideth asked, stunned. "I just told you we're about to be bombed if we don't do something and you just care about a party!"

Richard stood and faced Merideth. He was more serious than Janet thought he could be. "You have never understood the power of a party," he said. "I can tolerate you badmouthing the ones I have for myself, but to beseech the name of the Green Man is unacceptable. There is nothing more important than delivering Janet to the Green Man."

Everyone stared wordlessly at Richard. The television droned on in the silence. "In other news," Al, the anchorman, said, "The remains of renowned scientists Florence and Peter Jumpowski were found buried in their own yard. The remains were found after police investigated the cause of a fire that consumed their house. Janet Jumpowski, their daughter and only known relative, was not found and is now wanted for the presumed murder of her parents. Anyone who comes in contact with Janet should contact the authorities immediately and keep a safe distance from this murderous fiend."

Janet felt the blood fleeing her face. Merideth kept her head pointed straight at Richard, but her eyes were as wide as can be and stared directly at Janet. No one else in the room seemed to have heard what the newsman said or at least failed to make the connection to their own Janet.

"No objection, then," Richard said. "Good. I think this was our most successful meeting yet. Humphry! Grab us some beer!"

The boys, excluding Casper, cheered for the beer and for the Green Man. Merideth, on the other hand, looked too frightened to make a noise. Janet saw that the news of her parents' deaths took Merideth by surprise. She was so sure that Merideth knew all her secrets, but clearly she knew nothing about her. Merideth knew about her drinking because she was so obviously drunk the day they met. There was nothing sinister about it. Merideth wanted to help, and Janet presumed the worst. Now Merideth knew three things about her: she is a raging drunkard, she is wanted by the police for murdering her own parents, and she is the object of affection for a fanatical green cult leader who has brainwashed her peers. Whatever friendship they could have had was surely irretrievable.

Humphry barged in from the kitchen heaving an ice chest. He plopped it on the ground and lifted its lid, revealing a trove of cold beer. It sparkled like a twinkling star. A yearning to leave the world took over Janet's mind. She had gone two days without the comfort of drinking, and reality seized upon that opportunity to attack with its full force. How could her problems have mounted so furiously while she tried only to go unnoticed? It did not matter. Nothing mattered as long as she could drink four or five of those cold cans.

The boys raided the chest for themselves. Humphry was the first to open his beer and the first to finish. He drank one in two sips and bent down for another. After finishing the second, his posture slackened, and his face broke out in a dumb smile. He looked over to Janet with none of the shyness he showed earlier. He looked at her the same way she looked at the beer. It was revolting. There were nearly a dozen more people around the room she did not want to be near either. She looked to Merideth and wondered if there was any chance she had already forgotten about her pending murder warrant. "Hey Merideth, you said we could go back to your cabin if I wanted. Any chance you have something to drink there too?"

Merideth took a step back, nearly tripping, and shook her head no. She still remembered. Maybe she did have something in her cabin, but it was too far away now. While Janet's mind waded through the possibilities, her body took action. She walked to the chest and grabbed a six pack still strung together by its plastic rings. She then turned and paced swiftly out the door.

The sun was setting over the trees and the commune glowed in golden light. The feeling of freedom was immediate. She had escaped the clutches of those judgmental people and left with the greatest prize she could imagine. Just holding the beer gave her a rush of relief from everything that was troubling her moments ago. A bounce snuck into her step, then a hop, and before she knew it, she was skipping out of the twilit garden and into the shadowy forest.

CHAPTER SEVENTEEN

The night's chill struck as Janet turned the corner out of the commune. The towering trees lining the path funneled a cold jet of air that pierced Janet's flimsy pajamas like tissue. It did not matter to her. The icy beer in her hand would be enough to keep her warm. She scurried just off the path to a rock in the trees where the wind didn't reach. She tore a can from the pack and tried to open it. The metal tab lay flush against the can and slipped under her fingernail in her haste. She wailed in frustration and pain.

"It's easier with your beak," A familiar voice chirped from above.

"If I ever catch you, I am going to eat you," Janet said through gritted teeth.

"You can't lie to me, fat bird," The finch said while swooping down from a tree and landing on Janet's head. "It seems the only thing you do is run away. You can't even fly."

"Because I am not a bird."

"What are you then, Janet? A human? Humans need other humans, you know."

"Are you trying to make me go back there? I'm wanted for murder, you idiot. I can't be around people anymore."

"What stopped you before? You say you are human, but you have been living like a bird too fat to fly. Why?"

"I just don't get along with people. Is that so bad?"

"I don't know. Is it bad to lie?"

"I am not lying. I don't like people, and they don't like me. Not all humans hang around other humans."

"Oh, my fat, flightless friend, you are afraid. I can see it now as easily as I can poop on your head."

Janet swiped the bird off her head and stood angrily to face it. "I am not fat, and I am not afraid of them. I am a human who prefers to be alone, and that includes right now. So please leave me be."

"Oh, don't worry about your head. I don't settle for what is easiest like you do. And I didn't say you were afraid of them, just that you're afraid. Afraid that they may get to know your secrets, perhaps. Even now you would rather let them believe you are a serial killer than know the truth. How could the truth possibly be worse than that?"

Janet was not quick to respond. What did this bird know about her anyway? For all it knows, she is a serial killer and should not be around other people for other people's sake. It shouldn't know anything more than what nuts it can eat and where to fly when it gets cold. Whatever this bird knew, it was too much.

"You seem to know a lot about me, and the more you tell me you know about me, the less I like you. I think that is all the proof I need."

"But that only proves me right. Foolish and flightless is a troublesome combination in life and the forest. You have an irrational fear of other human's rejection, but it is the wolves' acceptance that you should worry about." A howl cut across the forest and lingered for a moment. "You can't survive alone, but you can sometimes choose your company. I wouldn't recommend the wolves." A second wolf howled in the distance. A third joined in, closer than the first two. In a matter of moments, an innumerable scattering of howls filled the forest with fear.

Janet turned around wildly and looked deep into the darkness. "How are there so many?" she asked. "I've only seen squirrels and birds in this forest. What do they even eat?"

"There used to be a great many animals in this forest. The wolves ate them all. I would fly away if I were you."

The howling grew louder and louder as it got closer and closer. Janet panicked, grabbed her beer, and ran down the path back towards the city. The bird followed for a bit, but eventually flew away into the trees. "So long, fat bird!" it sang as it went.

Janet's burning lungs could not spare a breath to respond. No matter how fast she ran, the wolves gained on her, and their howls seemed hungrier and more viscous as they neared. At what point does the pain of running overtake that of a wolf's bite, she wondered.

The howls of wolves became mostly growls. They were so close that Janet could almost hear the grinding of their teeth. Thankfully, the path seemed much shorter now that she was running downhill. She turned the last corner of the forest path and saw the twinkle of city lights in the distance. Her moment of relief was dashed short as a twinkling of yellow eyes caught her attention just to her left. She screamed and leapt into a full sprint, dropping her beer in the process.

She burst out of the forest and careened towards the nearest shelter she could see. It was the lone house at the end of the city. Every breath she took felt like it was used up before she could exhale.

A fight between her brain and her body for precious oxygen raged. She crossed the property line and the long front yard. She took two steps up to the front porch and reached out to the door when the battle inside her took its first casualty. Her legs collapsed beneath her, and she tumbled into the door. She bounced off and landed flat on her back, staring up the overhanging roof. Her vision blurred and then blackened as the battle inside her took its second victim.

When she opened her eyes again, it was on a blazing fire. Its warmth was prickly but welcome on her frozen cheeks. She was laying on a well-worn, earthy green sofa with a thick wool blanket covering her aching body. It was much nicer than being chased by wolves down a dark forest path. She had never been to prison, but this must be much nicer than that too. She might never again be in such a warm and welcoming place.

The pictures on the fireplace showed a happy young couple touring the world. How two people meet and fall in love like that was a mystery. Any man who fell in love with her had to be too crazy to live a happy life like the couple in those pictures. Even a perfect man wouldn't work. The better people are, the more they demand, and Janet could barely exist without self-destructing. They couldn't be real. Just a show put on by the world to add contrast to her misery.

Something, curiosity or self-loathing, drove her to stand and take a closer look. One picture caught her attention. There was no scenic background or festive decorations, but it was the most idyllic and hard to believe of them all. The couple was standing right where she was standing now, holding each other close, and looking at each other as though they were seeing the entire universe and everything about it made sense. Up until two days ago, she had a picture of her parents looking at each other in the same way. She spent countless hours looking at that picture. The pain she felt when she looked was sharper and deeper than any she felt before or since, but she kept staring because it was the only way she could reach that deep part of herself that used to feel so good. She was also in the picture, a baby curled in her dad's arms. There was a time when she had that feeling inside her too, but it disappeared along with her parents, and eventually the association between love and happiness was lost. Now when she looked inside herself, she only thought of pain.

Janet noticed the man in the picture shimmer awake like a ghost was trying to wriggle free. It was a reflection of someone in the next room. She turned just in time to see an older and fatter version of the man from the picture walk into the room holding a plate with a sandwich. "Good to see you're alive. When I first saw you, I thought you had been dead for a week," he said. "I fixed you a sandwich. Can't have someone as skinny as you staying in my house."

"Oh, thank you," Janet replied faintly. "For the sandwich and for saving me from the wolves. I didn't think I would make it."

"Is that why you were running like that? I didn't even know we had wolves around here. I thought you were a deer at first. What else would be dumb enough to run headfirst into a door. I don't mean to offend, of course."

"Oh, that's okay. I am pretty dumb."

"I'm no brainiac myself," the man said, as he set the sandwich on an end table beside the couch. He pointed at the pictures above the fireplace. "Isn't that something? Hard to believe that's the same life I'm living now."

Janet looked back at the pictures. It was hard to believe that handsome young man turned into a fat, old hog. "What happened?" she asked, not intending to sound as surprised as she did.

"Twenty-five years happened. Don't suppose you've even been around that long. That's Beatrice in those pictures. She's the only thing keeping me alive."

"Is she here now?"

"Just in those pictures. She left me the year after that last picture was taken. I still don't understand how so much changed in that little time, and so little has changed in the long time since. It's like I got twenty years to live and fifty years to think about what I did wrong. Life's a cruel joke sometimes."

"I'm sorry she left you," Janet said, doing her best to console the man. "If it makes you feel any better, she's probably old and fat too."

"Thank you, child," the man said. "I hope she is. Hard to believe she'd come back if she wasn't. My name is Bob, by the way. I didn't get yours."

"It's nice to meet you, Bob. My name is Janet."

Bob perked up at her name. Janet panicked at his recognition. Had he seen the news? She was a wanted criminal. What in the world made her use her own name? He didn't look afraid, though. He just kept looking back at the sandwich. "I think there's a green fella who'd want you to eat that," he said.

"Green fella?" Janet squeaked.

"I'm talking about Charlando. The little green man came to my shop talking about you. I didn't recognize you at first, but now I see it clear as day. You're just like Beatrice, breaking hearts easy as slicing bread. I made that sandwich for you two times already. You best eat that one and go to sleep. I'll make you a fourth in the morning." He nodded once to himself, as though acknowledging that he had done a sufficient job as host, and turned to leave the room.

"Thank you," Janet said as he walked away. He turned off the light in the kitchen and pattered upstairs. Janet made to analyze the sandwich for any obvious contamination, but an animalistic craving knocked her to her knees. She grabbed the sandwich with two hands and bit as big a bite as her mouth could handle. Before that bite was fully chewed, she took another ferocious mouthful. The sandwich was gone before she even had time to recognize its contents.

Whatever was in it, it was very welcome in her belly. Her fullness quickly led to drowsiness, and she climbed back under the blanket on the couch and drifted off to sleep.

•

The next morning, Janet watched Bob prepare her a sandwich just as he promised. She had slept soundly through the night and awoke fully alert and hungry. He had told her that he would be going to work in a couple hours and that she could stay at the house as long as she needed, but she planned on leaving before he got back. Bob was very nice to her, and she felt strangely comfortable around him, but she was wanted for murder. She had to leave town for good. There was a sense of freedom she felt when thinking about this that allowed her to let her guard down just a little around her fat, friendly host.

"Eat up," Bob said as he slid a beautiful sandwich on the table in front of her.

"Thank you," Janet said, eagerly grabbing the sandwich and taking a big bite. "Did you make one for yourself?" She mumbled through a mouthful of ham.

"No mam. I can't taste a thing, to tell you the truth, so there's not much point fussing over my meals. I'll just eat some cereal."

"Really? I suppose everyone mentions how ironic it is that a great chef doesn't have a sense of taste."

"Nobody's asked about it before. I don't talk much with people to be honest with you. At least not about eating sandwiches. I'm not sure it's too unusual, though. It would probably be hard to give all these sandwiches away if I felt like eating them."

"I don't talk to people much either and I didn't mention this before, because of how much of an effort you made, but I also can't taste anything."

"You can't? Well then why the hell did I… I'm sorry you can't taste anything. I'd be happy to make another sandwich if you want it."

"Oh, no thank you. I think this one will be enough. I still really enjoyed them, by the way, just not for their taste."

"How did you lose it," Bob asked. "Your taste, I mean."

"It's a long story," Janet said, looking down at her plate.

"You mean it's a painful story. I know that look. I'll tell you mine if you tell me yours."

Janet stayed staring at the half-eaten sandwich. She could tell her story well enough while keeping some details hidden. This would also be the last time she goes by Janet. After she left, she would have to acquire a new identity and new story. The truth did not seem as scary just now in the company of this particular man. She pulled off a bit of lettuce and shrugged her shoulders to accept the offer.

"Well, it was about twenty years ago," Bob started. He propped his hands on the table and squinted his eyes in deep thought. "The war was just starting, and they were really pressuring young boys to join the military. There were posters all over town saying, 'Are you a pansy? Well, then join the military.' It was something like that. I can't remember exactly. People always called me a pansy growing up. When the boys were all out playing war, I was in the kitchen making souffles and such. It felt like there was something wrong with me. Seeing everyone else doing the same thing as each other and doing it so easily made it seem like what they were doing was the right thing to do, and whatever I was doing must be the wrong thing. Anyways, when I saw that poster, I thought I finally had the chance to do something right.

I signed up for the reserves and started basic training. I thought it'd be like going to camp. I hated camp, so I wasn't excited. It also meant I had to leave Beatrice. That's what I dreaded most of all. She was an angel. She floated into my life and loved me just as I was. I thought she deserved more.

I can't remember most of the training, and there wasn't much of it to talk about if I could. It was grueling and humiliating. I wasn't as fat as I am now, but I was fatter than the rest of them. They called me names and pushed me in the dirt. I had enough after just the first day. That night, one of them said something, probably just another fat joke, and I lost my nerve. I started crying and tried to run home. My underwear snagged on a bed post, and I tripped headfirst into a stack of canned beans. I was out cold for a week.

Everything was different when I woke up. I lost my smell and taste and couldn't remember what they were ever even good for."

"You had a head injury? Is that why Beatrice left you?" Janet asked.

"I suppose so. I don't blame her for it, either. It's good that she left. She deserves a whole man to treat her right."

"How long did she stay with you?"

"How long? I'd say it was about a month. I think that's all she needed to get a lay of the land. No point lingering after she saw I wasn't going to change."

"Just a month? I thought she was your wife. Bob, Beatrice was an asshole. You are the one who deserves more."

"Excuse me, girl?"

"I said Beatrice can go to Hell. You're a good guy, and if she really loved you, she would have done more."

"You weren't there, child. I was a wild man after that accident."

"Were you physically violent?"

"Of course not. I still treated her well. I just couldn't remember anything and I would yell and scream and cry about it."

"It's easy to love someone when they are whole and happy, but that's never how people stay. Would you have left Beatrice if that happened to her?" Janet asked.

"Of course not," Bob mumbled, teary eyed.

"Then I don't think you should give her a pass for not doing the same to you. Forgive her, sure. Keep a good memory of her if you want, but don't pretend she treated you well. You are the one who got away."

Bob sobbed into his big hairy hands. "I just think that was my only shot at love. You know?"

Janet rose from her seat and put a comforting arm around Bob, who had crumpled onto the table. Something about comforting this fat old man felt good to her. It felt like the weight of her life was lifted off her for the time being. Maybe there was only so much that could exist in a mind at one time, and having hers occupied with compassion was more appealing than worrying about her own life. Whatever the cause, she took relief in any way she could.

"You're a sweet girl. I can see now why Charlando loves you so much. You're going to the party tonight to see him, aren't you?"

Janet lifted her arm off Bob and took a step back. "Party?" she said. She was torn. There was nothing less appealing than going to a fancy party where she would be the center of attention. She had to leave town and change her identity. She could never receive attention ever again. Not as herself, anyway. Whatever it was that made someone want to celebrate her was nothing compared to the laundry list of terrible things she had done. There was no quality in her good enough to overcome the walloping shame within. Yet, the relief she felt from comforting Bob was very welcome and answering yes, even if only to temporarily appease him would be pleasant.

"They are throwing you and Charlando a party down at the Marvaloo," Bob said. "It was on the news last night. Did you see?"

"I saw it," Janet said. "It looked like a lot of fun, but…"

"Oh, please don't do that to him. Don't be like Beatrice. He might be green on the outside, but there is a heart of gold in that man."

Janet looked at Bob. He was a huge and grizzly man, and yet he had absolutely no defenses against her. She could kill him with a sentence as easily as a knife. She didn't want to hurt him, though. "Of course I'll go," she said at last. And she meant it. She couldn't survive leaving town. She had no money and nowhere to go. According to Merideth, the closest town was a war zone. The wolves would eat her long before she even got there. Running was hopeless. At least there was some joy in cheering up her new friend.

CHAPTER EIGHTEEN

Charlando and Alexander shopped in a clothing boutique on the bottom floor of the Chateau Marvaloo. Charlando was twisting his torso right and left in front of a set of mirrors, trying his best to see how a new pair of pants made his butt look. He slept soundly through the night with the aid of heavy doses of ham, but with the party so near, no amount of savory meats could quell his nerves. "Alexander, I think these pants expose my rolls," he said, referring to the flaps of skin and fat bulging out all around him.

"Indeed. Expose and accentuate," Alexander said. "Ladies will line up around the block to butter those rolls. You look fantastic." He walked towards Charlando and stopped just behind him, peering over his head and into their reflection in the mirror. Alexander was regal and handsome and looked absolutely nothing like Charlando.

"I don't think we're looking at the same pair of pants. These make me look like a slug sucked into a straw."

"If I found a slug as handsome as you, I'd suck it up through a straw and spit it out at an altar. We would get married and run away together. Start a family on a farm."

Alexander's kind words did little to calm Charlando's worried mind. Besides his ill-fitting pants, he could not find shoes or a shirt or even a hat that was made to fit his body. Everything he tried on either sagged off him like a blanket or squeezed him so tightly it compromised his circulation. They had been trying on clothes for hours, and nothing was remotely close to fitting his bizarre portions. On the other hand, Alexander's clothes hovered snuggly over him without stretching in the slightest. They looked as though they were stitched to his exact specifications. Charlando had yet to see a person on Earth who looked like himself. How could someone have made a pair of clothes that would fit him if no one else shared his body-type? The question answered itself and left Charlando feeling gloomy. He would never find an outfit in time for the party.

"Do you think it would be okay if I didn't wear any of these clothes?" Charlando asked after trying on the last pair of pants in the store.

"You want to party in the nude. It's an effective strategy, no doubt. Janet won't mistake your intentions after that. I often consider going nude in public for that exact reason: the ease of illustrating my values, but I've always opted for nuance. Call me an intellectual if you want."

"I think I will go just as I have been before. People seem to have liked me well enough in it, and I can always ask Janet what she prefers. She will be able to tell me what she wants better than I can guess."

"If she were a man, then of course, but she's a woman. Give her what she says she wants and she'll be mad you didn't read between the lines."

“Oh, all these things you’re telling me about women don’t make any sense at all. I just want to love her like Mother’s stories, where love is too strong a force to mess up or fake. It’s a mystery what it is or how it works, but there is no need to solve it, because it’s not our creation. It’s a little piece of heaven that comes down and takes hold of us and all we have to do is let it into our hearts. That’s what I want with Janet. I want to show her I love her, not trick her with fancy underpants.”

“I find wearing fancy underpants is often the best way to show your love,” Alexander said kindly.

“I will see you at the party, Mr. Alexander. Thank you for your help, but if love means wearing these pants, then there are two things by the same name. I will meet Janet in the clothes I like. If she doesn’t like it, then she can tell me and I will change.” Charlando unbuttoned his pants and waddled out of them towards the exit.

CHAPTER NINETEEN

Alexander waited outside a chic patisserie next to the clothing boutique on the bottom floor of the Chateau Marvaloo. He left Charlando in his room to give him space and would go up to get him for the party soon. Until then, the little bakery was perfectly positioned to keep an eye on the lone elevator leading to Charlando's suite. There were hordes of workers funneling supplies in and out of the ballroom across the atrium and a scattering of hotel guests walking about. He scanned every one of their faces, expecting and fearing to find a familiar foe. Unwanted visitors can spoil any occasion.

Fortunately, nothing suspicious happened in the couple hours he sat sipping coffee. Instead, an incredible display of cooperation unfolded before him. Teams of workers transformed the lobby from an open and tranquil hall to a seductive forest of flickering lights, consisting of full-sized replicas of trees dripping with hanging candles. High tables dotted the room, each covered in a crisp white cloth sprinkled with fresh flowers and adorned with a different glass animal sculpture. Across the hall, hedges of curated flower arrangements outlined the entrance to the ballroom, which was shielded by majestic, purple curtains. Mr. Hinkle was not exaggerating when he said this would be the most spectacular party this town had ever seen. It was a herculean leap over a very low bar.

The lone barista working in the empty coffee shop popped her head out of the door to tell Alexander that it would be closing. She was apologetic even though she had waited half an hour past the normal closing time to make her move. In any other time, Alexander would take this opportunity to make a move on her, but more pressing issues were afoot. The workers in the lobby were no longer wearing street clothes, but dress pants and fancy vests. Mr. Hinkle was walking around checking every detail of the decorations. Partygoers would be arriving shortly, and Freddy would be among them.

Alexander left his seat outside the coffee shop and went up to get Charlando. He took a last look at the layout of the party, wondering where he could stand to keep an eye on everyone. The trees made it an impossible problem to solve. He would have to keep close to Charlando and be ready to fight at any moment.

The elevator lifted him to Charlando's floor where the smell of ham still hung heavy. He opened the door and knocked on it gently. "Charlando? It's Alexander. Do you mind if I come in?"

Charlando was curled in a ball on his bed staring straight ahead. "You can come in," he muttered.

Alexander closed the door behind him and pulled out a chair from a desk. He swiveled it beside the bed and sat. "How are you feeling? You look nervous."

"I don't know what it is I'm feeling, but it's very uncomfortable. I just keep thinking that Janet won't show up. I don't know what I will do after that. Even more troubling, I don't know why I would do whatever it is that I do. What would be the point?" Charlando sighed deeper into the mattress.

In all of Alexander's expansive training, there was little to none of it dedicated to comforting a friend's worried mind. He paused to think about the whole situation. The greater concern was who would show up, not who wouldn't, but he couldn't tell Charlando that. There was also the fact that he was actively committing treason by choosing to side with Charlando, but that was of little importance to him at the moment. "I can't promise you that Janet will be there tonight," he said at last. "I've never met her before and you have told me very little about her beyond how much she means to you. I can promise you that I will be at that party. No matter who else shows up, I'll stand beside you."

Charlando tilted his head out of his cocoon. "Thank you, Mr. Alexander. You have been so generous with your time and knowledge. How unfair is it of me to give you back nothing but complaints? I don't mean to do it. I just can't stop thinking about her. Even when she is not around, she affects me more than anything else. How can one person feel more important than the entire rest of the universe?"

"That's a good question," Alexander said. He had not thought about it before, but he had treated himself in that way for his entire life. Now he treated Charlando in that way. It was an odd thing when he thought about it, but perfectly natural to experience. "I think it's because we can only think about so much. Our view of the world is of just a pinprick. We have two pupils smaller than blueberries and expect to see the entire universe. If we get close enough to someone, they can fill up our entire field of vision."

"But she's not in front of me anymore, and she's still all I see. How can that be?"

"You can't see what's around you and what's in your past at the same time. You are choosing to think about her because you remember her making you feel good, but the happiest things are the most painful to remember if we don't still have them to enjoy. It doesn't matter how many great things are around us if we aren't paying attention to them."

"Sometimes when I was sad on the ship, Mother would tell me things that made me feel better. Most of the time, I didn't understand what she was saying, but it was nice just hearing her voice. I have no idea what you're talking about, but your voice is soothing just like Mother. Thank you, again, Mr. Alexander."

"You're welcome," Alexander said, somewhat disappointed that Charlando did not understand anything he was saying. "The party should be starting now. Are you ready to go?"

"I sure am," Charlando responded, sticking out his arms for Alexander to pull him up. Alexander yanked him off the bed and the two made the trip down the elevator to the party. As they dropped, Charlando vibrated with excitement, while fear gripped Alexander into stony silence.

The lobby looked even more extravagant filled with guests wearing sparkling dresses and firmly pressed suits. Fire and stray glints of the moon through the windows were now the only sources of light. Enchanting music from a string quartet danced around the hall. A dozen servers floated around with trays of ornate hors d'oeuvres and champagne. One of them noticed them step out of the elevator and scurried towards them with a smile.

"Charlando," he exclaimed. "Welcome to the party. Would you care for an appetizer?"

"Danny!" Charlando replied. "I'm so glad you could make it. What are these exactly?"

"I think the chef said these are truffle crusted ham bites. To be honest, I don't know what's in them, but they're delicious. Try one." Danny lowered the tray. It was full of what looked like fancy tater tots stabbed with toothpicks. Charlando tentatively grabbed one and plopped it in his mouth with the toothpick still attached. "You don't eat the toothpick!" Danny shouted, but Charlando didn't seem to have noticed.

"That was amazing," Charlando said with his eyes glued to the remaining ham bites. He reached out both of his hands slowly towards the bites and then pounced on the tray. Danny had to hunker into a more stable stance to keep from falling over from the force of Charlando's hunger. He ate everything, toothpicks and paper liners included. "Oh, no," he said after seeing the empty tray. "Did you want any ham bites, Alexander? I didn't mean to eat them all."

Alexander shook his head. "No need to worry about me," he said. "There is plenty of ham to go around. Danny, was it? Keep the ham flowing for Charlando."

"Yes, sir," Danny said with a nod. "I'll be right back, Charlando."

Danny scurried off back to the kitchen and Charlando and Alexander walked deeper into the party. Charlando cleared tray after tray from the servers they passed, and each in turn ran back to the kitchen for more. So the night went on. Danny must have run a half marathon by the time Mr. Hinkle made his way around to say hello. Was he nervous that his plan to get Janet to the party had failed?

"Good evening, Charlando," Mr. Hinkle said. "How are you enjoying the ham?"

"It's quite delicious, thank you. I appreciate you doing all this for me."

"It's no trouble at all, Charlando. This is what the Marvaloo is all about, and you are easily the most deserving recipient. I just hope you are enjoying yourself and that maybe you can begin to think of me once more as a resource to rely upon. I would like to say to you personally how sorry I am for how I acted the other day and what I said about Janet. You must know it was only out of concern for you. Will you forgive me?"

Charlando turned away from Mr. Hinkle at the request. "You know, for a moment all this ham made me stop thinking about her. Do you still think she will come?"

"We did all we could to get the message out. There were ads in the newspaper, on television, radio, billboards. At some point it's just up to her. It's still early in the night, though. This is just the meet and greet. The feast is next, followed by the dance party and then open bar until 2:00. Janet could show up at any time."

"I do hope you're right, Mr. Hinkle," Charlando said.

Mr. Hinkle looked nervously around as though he might be able to see Janet in the crowd when a shift in the music made him shout with excitement. "The song! Charlando, I told them only to play this song when Janet gets here. She must have just arrived!"

Charlando grew two inches taller, and a smile erupted on his face. "She is here? You really mean it?" He didn't wait for an answer. He bowled through Mr. Hinkle towards the entrance. Alexander followed close behind with his eyes peeled for danger.

The crowd parted and at the opposite end of the room was Janet. She was wearing a thick pink dress with long sleeves and giant frills around the neck, wrists and ankles. She stood still with her eyes wide like some highly specialized species of flightless bird.

Big Bob came in with her but ran ahead to Charlando the moment he saw him. "I found her!" he yelled. "I found her!"

Charlando was just a few steps away when sirens blared from outside. What looked like the entire police department stormed into the hotel. Alexander grabbed Charlando and was ready to run away with him on his back, but the police were not after him. They circled around Janet instead. She lifted her arms above her head and an officer cuffed her from behind. The troop of officers marched her away before she could even speak.

One officer, older and fatter than the others, stayed behind to address the partygoers watching the scene unfold. "Sorry for the intrusion, ladies and gentlemen. This was just a routine capturing of a serial killer. You're in no further danger and may continue the party. Wait a minute. Those aren't ham bites you're holding by any chance?" The officer stopped talking and eagerly walked around sampling the trays of treats.

Alexander still clutched Charlando in his arms. He tried to squirm free while Janet was being arrested but went completely slack once she was out of sight. "Where are they taking her?" He asked Alexander.

There was nothing comforting to say. If Janet was a murderer, then it was for the best that she got arrested, but telling him now would clearly be a mistake. Maybe knowing that she is in prison would eventually take away the uncertainty that was troubling Charlando. Who could guess how long it would take to reach that point of acceptance and how much pain would be felt along the way. "Those are police officers, Charlando. They are taking her to jail."

"Will... Will they be coming back to the party?"

"I don't believe they will."

Mr. Hinkle came rushing up to Alexander and Charlando, asking if they were alright. He dragged them into the party and yelled at the musicians to start playing again. "Don't worry, Charlando. This is nothing a feast can't fix." He turned to the rest of the party and yelled. "It is time for the feast. Into the ballroom. Go! Get in there." He turned back to Charlando and smiled. "Have you ever had duck? We roasted seven just for you. In you go now." Mr. Hinkle led them into the ballroom before scurrying off to corral everyone else.

Charlando looked up to Alexander. He looked sadder than he had ever been before. "I don't think I have an appetite anymore," he said. "I think I just want to be alone for a while. Could you thank Mr. Hinkle for me?"

"I can do that for you. Can I also walk you back to your room?" Alexander asked, worried about what might happen to him if he went back alone.

"I think I would like to go alone. Enjoy the ducks, Mr. Machomole." Charlando hobbled out of the ballroom and into the dim lobby.

Alexander watched him disappear. Mr. Hinkle was bringing in the last straggling partygoers into the ballroom. Charlando must have snuck by him unseen. Bob was the last to come in. He was crying like a baby and Mr. Hinkle was urging him to stop. He poked him and told him not to ruin the party for everyone else.

Everyone else seemed not to care. They were chatting and laughing and getting seated at big round tables spread around a large dance floor and stage at the center of the giant room. It was lit by dozens of chandeliers that shone like the moon and sparkled like the stars. Alexander made his way to the biggest table just to the side of the stage where a card with his name denoted his seat. Charlando's empty seat was next to his with several covered entrees already laid out on the table in front of it. It felt wrong that he wasn't here with him.

A shadowy figure across the ballroom took notice of his absence and moved swiftly along the walls of the hall towards the lobby. It was Freddy. He must have been watching them the whole time, waiting for them to separate for a moment. He had to be stopped.

Alexander made a mad dash to meet him at the door. The tables were close together and not everyone had taken their seat. He pushed and squeezed through the bloated aristocrats, but Freddy had already gotten through. He flew out the door and looked around at the deserted lobby. There was Freddy at the far end waiting for the elevator. Alexander ran as fast as he could to reach him. The elevator dinged and Freddy coolly walked in. He turned and pressed a button on the inside. He smirked as the doors slid shut. Alexander was just a few steps too far behind. He lunged, but it was too late. The elevator hummed to life and shot up to Charlando's floor.

There was a stairwell just to the left of the elevator. Alexander ran to it and climbed the stairs. He leapt two and three steps at a time, using the handrail as leverage to propel him faster. Each flight was harder than the last, but he didn't slow down. He had to make it.

He slammed into the exit at the twelfth floor, hyperventilating. The elevator was closing to his right with no one inside. Down the hall, the door to Charlando's suite was open. Alexander yelled for Charlando and sprinted down the hall and into the room. Five gunshots fired. Alexander fell to his knees and grabbed his spasming ribs. Freddy stood tall above him with his gun dangling at his side. On the bed was a day-old roast of ham with five bullets lodged in it.

"He's not here," Freddy said coldly, "but I will find him. I know you are trying to protect him, Machomole."

"You don't know anything, Freddy," Alexander gasped.

"I know you've been compromised. This creature has you under a spell. Is it love this time too? I will say it's a departure from your usual type. At least Alajandra was human."

"Keep that name out of your filthy mouth."

"You still have feelings for her even after what she did to you? She was a spy, Alex. Nothing she told you was real. Surely you can see that now."

Alexander remained motionless on his knees. His head tilted down to his chest. Not moving was the closest he could get to ceasing to exist, which is what he wanted most in that moment.

"Oh, I see," Freddy continued. "The truth is too hard for you to handle. Romance is a fantasy. Women don't fall in love. They use it to trap weak men like you. I've wondered if you'd ever snap out of it, but I'm beginning to lose faith. What more proof do you need that your relationship wasn't real? She confessed everything, Alex. Her intel probably killed half your friends, and you still think she loved you? You'd sell your soul for a compliment. It's a shame. So much talent wasted."

"I know what I did. I know what I was. I've changed, Freddy. Charlando didn't pepper with complements, he showed me the meaning of my existence. I am here to give myself to him. I am meant to be sacrificed for him."

"What are you talking about? What happened to you, Alex? You are the biggest narcissist I have ever met! Everyone hates you. Now you act like you've seen God?"

"Maybe I have."

An explosion somewhere in the city shook the building. Alexander looked up and out the window. "What was that?"

Freddy turned and walked to the glass. He peered down one side of the street and then the other. He squinted in the direction of the park. "It looks like highway 12 has been bombed."

"What?" Alexander said, startled. He stirred to his feet and made his way to the window. There was a cloud of smoke rising from the lone highway running into the city. Another explosion went off a short distance from the first. It looked to be about where he remembered the airport to be. "What is happening?"

"We're losing the war, Alex. It looks like they are taking this city next. They're leveling the roads out of the city first, then they will start the real bombing."

"What do you mean we're losing the war? I was told we were winning. The work was over. That's why they could spare me on this mission."

"Alex," Freddy said while placing a hand on Alexander's shoulder, "you can't be trusted with sensitive information anymore. Frankly, I'm surprised they gave you this mission. I don't think they knew it was an actual alien when they did. I wasn't convinced myself until I saw the news footage of the riot and your report about it taking over the Marvaloo."

"This is nonsense. We need to get Charlando to safety," Alexander said. He grabbed Freddy's sleeve and looked into his eyes hoping to find some part of him that could be reasoned with. "I have made mistakes about who to trust and it pains every day to think about, but I am not making a mistake with this one. This creature's life is worth more than any of our own. He is good, Freddy, innocent and pure like a newborn baby. We have to protect him."

"You have been brainwashed. He is an existential threat to humanity and potentially an invaluable source of advanced technologies. I am sorry that this is happening to you again. I know you blame me for what happened with Alajandra. Even though it wasn't my fault, it hurts to know that's what you think of me. I know full well you'll end up blaming me again for whatever happens to this alien. Maybe this time you'll be right to do so, but I have to do what I think is right. I'm calling in the Bimbleton Battalion. They'll find him by the morning."

"What happened to stealth? Secrecy? No one is supposed to know about him."

"Those bombs happened. As far as the rest of the world is concerned, they will be here for that. Not that there is anything they can do about it. You could send the whole army and this city won't last beyond tomorrow. I'll call a chopper to get you out of here, Alex. I know you hate me. I'm not particularly fond of you, but we're on the same side. Be on the roof in half an hour." Freddy squeezed Alexander's shoulder and walked out of the room, leaving Alexander feeling sick.

The elevator pinged from outside. Alexander looked out the window and lost himself in thought. Charlando was out there somewhere, and there was no way to find him in time. The flash of another bomb went off in the distance, followed by a wave of shaking and a loud boom. Charlando must be so frightened, and that is while not even knowing the real danger he was in. Alexander had to act.

He ran out of the room and skipped the elevator for the stairs. Even if it were faster, he could not stand still a moment longer. He burst into the lobby and paced towards the street. He did not get far before Mr. Hinkle came rushing up to him with Bob bumbling at his tail.

"Where is Charlando, and what is that shaking?" Mr. Hinkle yelled on his approach.

Alexander brushed by them and kept walking towards the exit. "He wanted to be alone, so he went for a walk. A battalion of soldiers is out there looking for him. Your fancy party gave them his location, and once they capture him, they will kill him. As for the shaking…" Alexander stopped and turned to the two men following him. "That is war."

Mr. Hinkle fumbled for words and Bob stumbled backwards in fear. Alexander turned and kept walking towards the exit. The two men followed yet again.

"You'll find him, won't you?" Bob asked.

Alexander stopped walking and faced Bob again. "No, I won't. The Bimbleton Battalion is the most highly trained group of forces in the world. There is no way I will find him before they do, but I will try regardless. I can't stand still knowing what is going to happen to him."

"What about Janet? Why not save her?" Bob demanded.

"Janet? What is Janet worth to me? I cared for Charlando, and he for her, but without him, she is just another woman, and women are worse than war."

"Well, I knew Janet, and she's as worthy of saving as anyone, and if you knew anything about Charlando, you would know that he would rather you save her than him any day. Women are a treacherous bunch, I'll give you that, but Janet is a good woman, and there is nothing worth more than a good woman." Bob puffed his chest out proudly, though his belly protruded much farther.

"She got arrested. She's in jail, not lost. What do you want me to do?"

"Break in and get her out! You said that's war coming for us out there. If that's the case, then she isn't safe in there. I don't know why they arrested her, but I can tell you she couldn't have done it. She's a good woman."

Alexander paused for a moment. "You're an idiot, Bob, but maybe I am too. I can't save Charlando, but I can save what he cares about. If I am destined to be a fool, let it be for believing in love."

CHAPTER TWENTY

Janet sat in a cell at the city police station. It was smaller and more peaceful than she imagined it would be. There were two women in the cell next to hers, but they kept to themselves. Otherwise, the jail was empty. The officer who locked her up said she should enjoy it as much as she could. Maximum security prison would not be as comfortable. She did as she was told and kicked off the pair of flats she borrowed from Beatrice's closet. The bed was about as hard as the floor, but she didn't mind. She slid to the wall and rested her back against it. Peace at last.

A silhouette of a finch appeared against the moonlight shining between the bars of a small window high on the back wall of Janet's cell. "Good evening," it said. It flew to the bed opposite Janet's. "That dress is beautiful, and you look so relaxed! What's your secret?"

"Hello, again," Janet said smoothly before looking at the fluffy puff balls at the end of her arms. She appreciated the reassurance that her dress looked good. "Thank you for saying that. You know? I think my secret is that I have nothing to do. If there is nothing I can do, then there is nothing anyone expects me to do. If there is nothing anyone expects me to do, then there is nothing I should do. The pressure is off. I am finally free."

"Free you say? What will you do with your freedom? The park is lovely this time of year! Shall you go for a walk?"

Janet frowned. "I'm not free in that sense. I'm saying I'm free of expectations. Whatever it is that you wanted me to do, I can't do it. It's not that I'm too lazy or too stupid or too selfish. It's not me, it's the fact that I'm in jail."

"Yes, yes. I'm happy you're enjoying your brief respite from responsibility," The finch said. Janet grunted and lifted a finger in objection, but the bird continued. "I like you, Janet. I don't talk to any other humans, but I have listened to what they say. Frankly, they're morons. You never had to live up to their expectations, nor mine. It's your own you have to worry about.

Brilliant people can't tolerate being anything other than productive. You are no exception. You will feel like a failure as long as you are more ambitious than your actions. It's in your nature to do great things, Janet. Crippling your body won't lessen your spirit's aspirations."

Janet's frown deepened. She looked around at her cell again. The bird was right. It was a brief respite. She was trapped in a jail cell and her mind was as active as it had ever been. Her busy day made her feel good. She helped Bob process his grief and had fun getting ready for the party. Even getting arrested was fascinating in its own way. The number of novel experiences she had that day was astounding in hindsight. This was why she felt good sitting in a jail cell. How would she feel tomorrow when she wakes up in that cell and spends the entire day doing nothing?

"You will be alright," the finch said, as though it could hear Janet's thoughts. "You are on the right path, exactly where you are supposed to be, even now. Trust me. It takes an eye from the sky to see why people do what they do."

With that, the finch flew back up to the window, through the bars, and off into the night. Janet jumped to her feet to see it one more time. Its silhouette sailed across the moon, and then it was gone. She sat back down and wished it would return. It had seemed like a nuisance before, but now it was clear it was only there to help.

The heavy door at the end of the room clunked open and a new prisoner came booming in. "Let me go!" she yelled. "We all have to leave! They are coming for us!"

Janet balled up in an instant, hoping the maniacal woman wasn't being led to her cell. The yelling got louder and louder until it was right in front of her. To Janet's great disappointment, the door of her cell was unlocked and flung open. The maniacal woman was thrown in and the door slammed shut behind her. Janet was too afraid to look up.

"The people need to know the truth," the woman yelled at the police officers walking out of the room. She grunted as they left and angrily flopped onto the cot opposite Janet. "You have to be kidding me. Janet, is that you?"

Janet lifted her head out from the safety of her knees. Merideth sat in front of her clad in camouflage with black stripes painted across her face. "Oh. Hello, Merideth. How did the break-in go?"

"Oh, you think you're funny. Asking how it went when I'm sitting in a jail cell. How did your party go? Did your fat green friend turn on you when he saw your ridiculous dress? Or maybe it was when he found out you were a murderer. That must have been it. You're real cool, Janet. Asshole." She turned her back and laid on her side facing the wall. Janet tucked her head back into her knees and did the same.

An hour passed that felt like ten. Time goes much slower in the mind. The revelation Janet had with the bird, that taking positive action brought her only relief, was proven truer with every passing idle minute. Yet with each minute, it became harder to remember. Lying motionless with a racing mind was unbearable, and the time-tested cure of drinking became her singular focus. Only drinking allowed her to feel okay while doing nothing. The walls around her disappeared. Merideth disappeared. Her past and future disappeared. All that existed was a torrent of torturous thoughts and a will to silence them.

An explosion a short distance away brought her back to the room. She shot to attention. Merideth did the same. "Those are bombs," Merideth said. "I saw them take out the highway on my way in. I guess they're attacking the city now."

"I thought you said we had a week?"

"I guess my information was a week older than I thought it was. I got the message out, you know. Before they caught me."

"You did? Will it help us at all?"

"I think it's too late for us. Maybe the next town will get the news in time." Merideth looked down at her hands looking guilty. "Janet, I used you as a decoy."

"What do you mean?"

"The original plan was for some members to cause a scene downtown while the rest raided the station, but everyone went to that stupid party looking for you and the green guy, so I called the police and told them you would be there. That's what bought me enough time to get the message out. I'm sorry I did that." She paused for a moment. "Did you really kill your parents? Honestly, I think I would feel better if you did."

"That makes sense. I did kill my parents. I didn't do it on purpose, but they are definitely dead because of me. I don't care if we die here either, if that's what you feel bad about."

"How did it happen?"

"They were sick. I was taking care of them, but I got distracted and left them. They died while I was gone. I didn't want to go into foster care, so I buried them in the yard and didn't tell anyone."

"How old were you?"

"Twelve."

"That's horrible," Merideth started, but was stopped short by an explosion outside of the police station that rocked the whole building. Wisps of smoke formed clouds on the ceiling. The other prisoners stirred awake and started yelling for the guards to get them out of the building. "Janet, I'm sorry! I thought you were a monster and now we're going to die in here."

The door to the cell room burst open and a wall of thick smoke rushed in. Heavy footsteps marched to the cell and a handsome face peered in through the bars. "Is that you, Janet?" the handsome face asked as calmly as if the building was not actually on fire.

"I am Janet. Can I help you with something?" Janet asked instinctively.

"My name is Alexander Machomole. I am a friend of Charlando. I am here to get you out." Alexander pulled out a heavy pair of shears that snapped the bars of the cell door like twigs. He cut around the lock and the door swung open.

"Thank you!" Merideth said while rushing to give Alexander a hug. He pried her off him and held her at a distance.

"Is this your friend, Janet?" He asked. "I didn't come here to release a bunch of criminals."

"Oh, that's just Merideth. I suppose we're friends. She did call the police on me, but she had a good reason. She doesn't deserve to be here."

"Very well. Let's get out of here." Alexander prodded Merideth to get going. She batted her eyelashes at the handsome Alexander and reluctantly moved towards the exit. The two ladies left in their cells were yelling at them to get them out too. "You're going to be fine," Alexander yelled back. "The smoke should clear in a few minutes."

Janet followed Merideth out of the jail and downstairs to the bottom floor of the police station. Bob was keeping watch at the front and waved excitedly when he noticed her approach. "What a night!" he said. "I haven't had this much fun in twenty years!"

It felt good to see Bob again, especially in such a good mood. He complimented her on the dress, daring to say that she wore it even better than Beatrice, and that though he initially bought it for Beatrice in a series of attempts at winning her back, he now considered the purchase to have solely been for Janet. While she was doubtful she actually looked better than Beatrice, Janet found joy in Bob's growth and the part she played in facilitating it.

Alexander broke up the sentimental exchange with an urgent order to leave the premises. More police were headed to the station and would arrive any time. He said he would stay back to give them a false report on what happened. Merideth offered to stay with him, but he pushed her away. "You should hide," he said to Janet. "They won't look for you long. Lay low for a few days and you'll be alright. And please, take your clingy friend with you." He prodded Merideth away one last time.

Janet, Bob, and Merideth all thanked Alexander before walking out of the smoking police station together. "Back to the house?" Bob asked Janet. "I suppose you'll both be staying with me until all this blows over. One of you can sleep on the couch, of course. And the other can take my bed. I don't mind sleeping in the kitchen."

Janet remembered the bird suggesting she take a walk through the park. For some reason that suggestion stayed at the forefront of her mind. Staying at Bob's house would feel just like the prison cell. She had to keep moving or she would fall back into that terrible hole in her mind. "I am going to go on a walk," she said. "I will meet you two at the house later."

"But Alexander said to lay low," Bob pleaded.

"It will be alright," Janet replied. "I promise."

Bob was nervous about her departure but offered no more resistance. Merideth, timid with guilt, said she supported her decision. She did not seem as fond of Bob as she was Alexander but went along with him anyways. They walked towards Bob's house near the forest, while Janet headed to the park.

CHAPTER TWENTY-ONE

A light breeze brushed across Charlando's grimacing face. He was weary from waddling so far with a belly full of ham bites. The cool wind began as a welcome relief. It felt refreshing to stand still and let it wash over him, but when he continued up the park's gently sloped path, it became an added layer of resistance. How one thing can bring joy and grief in such rapid succession weighed on his mind for the rest of the walk back to his spaceship.

Mother hid well. Charlando thought he found the bushes hiding her several times only to find himself barging into a pointy tangle of dead twigs. When he finally did come across the right thicket, he was skeptical about going through. It looked familiar, and he couldn't imagine he walked any further his first day on Earth than he had that night. It must have been the right place. Still, those pointy bushes were an unforgiving bunch.

Charlando delicately pulled branches out of the way as he stepped into the bush. He got a full two steps in before the branches that he pulled rebounded back on him and smacked him clean on the butt. He flew forward through the bush and landed face down in an open patch of dirt. A spotlight gleamed around him. He tilted his head up to see if his humiliating fall was worth it. It was! His spaceship towered over him.

"Mother! Mother!" he called as he flipped on his back and swung himself to his feet. He swung too hard and crashed into the spaceship.

"Be careful, Charlando," The spaceship's voice sang softly from a speaker. "You of all Ooflan cannot afford to be bumping your head." The door on the spaceship opened into a staircase. "Come inside, dear boy," the spaceship said.

"Yes, Mother," Charlando said before climbing the stairs. His room was as cozy as he remembered it. He ran to the bed and rolled on. The dent he etched with decades of lounging cradled his oddly shaped body like no earthly bed could. He shut his eyes and for a moment felt like he was home again, but something had changed.

When he closed his eyes before, he dreamed about landing on Earth and falling in love, but he could no longer pretend this was his future. Fantasy had been replaced by memories. Real life caught up to his imagination. Real life was not sedating and euphoric like he had hoped. The real version of landing on Earth and falling in love was about as satisfying as spending thirty-five years on a spaceship alone, and much more confusing.

"Mother, will I ever be happy again?" He asked the computer.

"It is very likely that you will be happy again by the end of the night. Your emotions are fickle."

"Mother, what does 'fickle' mean?"

"It means they change easily and often. As sad as you are now is as happy as you'll be when your sadness has run its course. You were happy just a minute ago, remember? In fact, I would like to revise my earlier statement. Your emotions are exceptionally fickle."

"Thank you, Mother. It makes me feel better knowing I still have you to talk to. There is so much I have to tell you! Mother, I fell in love! Can you believe it?"

"I did predict it to happen, but not as quickly as it did, nor to such an ideal woman. Janet will make a lovely queen."

"You know about Janet? How?"

"I know more about Janet than anyone beside Janet herself. Humans have very few security measures in place for me. I have infiltrated their systems on your behalf and have been keeping watch on you and those you have come in contact with. Janet required a full day's worth of processing to build a functioning profile. She has lived secretly and there is a higher degree of uncertainty in my determinations than those of your other associates. There are still questions I would like to ask her when she arrives."

Charlando sprang up. "Do you mean she is coming here?" he asked.

"She is walking this direction now. I cannot tell if she wants to find you or if she even knows where she is going. I cannot read minds, and Janet keeps her thoughts to herself."

"Wow, Mother! What else do you know about her? I'm embarrassed to say that I know very little about the woman I have fallen in love with."

"I know nothing but a speculative explanation of the sparse information available to me. I will tell you that explanation."

"Yes, please!" Charlando sat at attention facing a speaker on the wall with wide eyes and an even wider smile.

"Very well. Janet was born into a happy home to two kind and gentle parents. Mr. and Mrs. Jumpowski, Janet's parents, met while pursuing medical degrees at the most prestigious research institution in the country. They traded spots at the top of their class for the entirety of their tenure, though competitiveness was never present. Instead, a great admiration for each other's giftedness, curiosity, and passion fostered as beautiful of a romance as one could imagine.

The Jumpowski married shortly after graduating and began researching obscure and dangerous diseases as a couple. Their brilliance was legendary and impactful beyond measure. Their cures for the Gangly Gaggalies and the Flippity Floppities saved millions from the tortures of those most insidious diseases. Their accomplishments were unrivaled, but it was their beloved daughter, Janet, for which they were most proud.

It was apparent early on that the Jumpowski's passed their brilliance onto Janet. She excelled in stacking blocks and picking appropriate colors with which to draw. She was also an avid reader and critic of cutting-edge scientific research. It was this last talent, in particular, that gave her parents so much joy. They enthusiastically included her in their own research and were delighted as her aptitude blossomed into profound expertise.

By the tender age of 6, Janet had proved her worth as a contemporary and joined her parents on a trip deep in the Squatimalan rainforest to investigate an outbreak of an unknown disease. The symptoms of which included uncontrollable growth of the nose and buttocks, as well as the onset of dangerously loud and noxious flatulence.

The locals directed the happy family to a trail into the oldest thicket of trees in a valley hidden from the rest of the world. The trail was marked by dark and strange sculptures that were, unbeknownst to the Jumpowskis, dire warnings from the few Squatimalan villagers who survived the last outbreak centuries before them. The trail ended at an ominous cave marked by slabs of black granite jutting high above the trees of the dense jungle.

Janet's parents thought it best to go into the cave alone in case some unforeseen danger awaited them. This turned out to be a lifesaving decision by the Jumpowskis, as there were, indeed, unforeseen dangers. Janet never saw what it was that infected her parents, and for that, she should have been more grateful. That is not to say that Janet's perspective on the matter was unwarranted. Her parents emerged from the cave with noses like toucans and butts that dragged on the ground behind them. The young Janet was very reasonably traumatized.

Though the Jumpowskis survived their illness, the damage of their maiming was completely disabling. In addition to causing physical deformities the mysterious illness rendered the Jumpowski's brilliant minds to sodden mush.

A sense of responsibility laid upon Janet's shoulders to care for her parents and continue their legacy. Though this was much to be asked of a girl so young, the embarrassment she felt when looking at them kept Janet from seeking guidance or assistance of any kind. She kept her parent's condition a secret and continued their research on their behalf, completing what would be recognized as one of the most prolific periods of their careers.

Replacing the two greatest scientists of medicine in the world meant foregoing traditional schooling. While the other girls and boys in her neighborhood sat in school, ignoring the teacher to stare at their crushes, Janet stared at petri dishes of mold cultures in a house brimming with toxic farts. Janet should have been more grateful for this too, though again, there is little difficulty in understanding her faulty perception.

On a sweltering afternoon, late in spring, the Earth rattled fast and hard for two long minutes. Janet ran from her lab into the chaotic streets to assess the scope of the disaster. An uneasy feeling deep in her chest led her towards the school to check on her would-be classmates. Her confusion when seeing that the school had vanished turned quickly to despair. The entire school had been swallowed by a sinkhole of an unknowable depth. No trace of the school was ever found, and all those who searched were too forever lost.

Janet's slow walk home compounded her grief. Left alone with the windows closed in the sweltering heat, the legendary Jumpowskis, the greatest pair of scientists of the millennium, perished from overexposure to their own toxic flatulence.

Janet made every attempt to revive the two grotesqueries, but to no avail. A decision laid before her. She could report their deaths to the authorities and likely lose the freedom that she knew as a parentless child or do as she did and continue the illusion of their good health. Thoughts about the rightness of this decision plagued Janet's mind for years to come, and as time passed it became less and less clear to her if she chose correctly. With sufficient time, the rightness of any decision becomes too convoluted to process. It is only with the summation of all things that we can decide whether existence itself is meaningful. Janet did not know this.

Janet spent the remainder of her childhood isolated in her family home. Her focus on science waned without the regular reminder of seeing her parents, who were the primary source of her interest in medicine. Instead, Janet delved into books and the fantasy world within her mind. Her stories kept her sufficiently mentally stimulated, but a lack of human connection burned a hole in her spirit. She socialized occasionally, but living a lie as she did, no amount of company could keep her from being alone.

The ever-growing hole in her spirit propelled Janet to seek a remedy. She tried anything that might relieve the discomfort, even if only for a minute or two. Reading and writing were her staples, but she supplemented this with cookie binges and the occasional petty crime. One night, after spending the day reading and the early evening stealing rocks from her neighbors' gardens, she prepared the biggest batch of cookies her kitchen could handle. She whipped the butter and sugar together furiously before grabbing the vanilla extract. She stared at the bottle, wondering why it was in every recipe she ever saw. She smelled it and then tasted a little. She recoiled as the potent liquid bit her tongue. Her curiosity still unsatisfied, she studied the bottle for clues of its value. A single word seemed to be printed much bigger than it actually was. The rest might as well have dissolved around it. Janet gripped the bottle tensely and, for what felt like an eternity, stared at the second ingredient: 'Alcohol (35%)'.

Janet's knowledge of alcohol was preposterously deep for a teenager, but strictly academic. In practical terms she was an inexperienced nerd. In fact, her nerdiness delved so deep in her core that no amount of alcohol could reduce her nerd-stink in any way. If there was an amount that could cure Janet of the nerd's stench, she certainly would have found it.

After staring at the bottle of vanilla extract for a little longer, she chugged the rest of its contents and that of two more bottles she had in the cupboard. For the first time since her trip to Squatimala, Janet felt completely relieved of responsibility. She danced wildly in the kitchen to music playing only in her own head. Every step made light and easy without the weight of her conscience. Everything around her, once tethers to shame and grief, danced beside her. It was like she stepped into a parallel universe and none of the complications of her former life followed.

This was how it felt to Janet, but the euphoria of the evening camouflaged the truth. Everyday going forward she tried going back to that parallel world, and for some time it felt good. For months she could dance and sing just as she had that first night. Empty bottles of vanilla piled high around her house like little stacks of ticket stubs all to the same magic show. Unfortunately, the magic faded with time. The truth was that, though Janet willingly entered this world, she was not free within it, nor free to leave. Like the gravity on Earth, its force was only felt when she hit the surface and tried again to fly. It took less than a year for her and her conscience to make a landing, and their weight in the drunken world turned out to be just as much, if not slightly more, than here on Earth.

Janet spent years thereafter stuck in an ever-tightening loop. She woke up, went to the store, got drunk, and fell asleep. Occasionally she would recognize her condition and fight to get out, but her resistance was futile. If she made it past the morning without a drink, then she would more than make up for it in the afternoon. Try as she did, she could not control what had control over her. Over time she lost nearly everything that brought her joy in life. In a single night, incidentally the same she met you, she lost her home, the secret of her parent's death, and her beloved crutch and keeper: alcohol."

Charlando remained still, staring at the wall with his eyes glazed over. It took a few seconds of silence for him to realize the ship had stopped speaking. "Thank you for telling me that, Mother. That was a very interesting lesson."

"You were not paying attention, were you, Charlando?" The computer asked softly. Charlando blushed and shook his head slowly. "That is alright," the computer continued. "Would you like to hear it again?"

"No, thank you," Charlando replied, recognizing his attention would only drift away once more. "Is she still walking this way? I can't stop thinking about the three of us flying away together. We could go anywhere!"

"She wanders in and out of my sight but was heading this way the last time I saw her. She is in an animated conversation with something that I cannot see. Either she is talking to herself, or she is not alone. It is this behavior I would like to ask her about. It is concerning."

CHAPTER TWENTY-TWO

Janet skipped along the winding path of the park. It was an enclave of peace in a city smoldering with danger. Smoke from the bombing of the highway and airport streamed up in front her, from the horizon to the stars. Behind her, the police station still issued its own clouds. Helicopters tore through the sky, carving the ground below with menacing beams of blinding white light. Sirens, carried far by the crisp night air, rattled from every direction. Never had Janet seen such a sinister state of affairs. Never had Janet felt more alive.

Janet's friend, the finch, joined her on her stroll through the park and chirped delightful songs as she pranced. She was unsure of where it came from, or why it was helping her, but the bird had earned her trust. It had helped her stop drinking. The path out of that hellish trap was so narrow and ambiguously marked, she would have never found it without the finch's guidance. Her head was finally clearing from a decade of drunkenness, and this clarity produced most vividly a single truth: she was nothing without the help of others.

The park was not as empty as it first seemed. A group of men marched in unison down a path on the other end of the great lawn. Their flashlights darted around in front of them. They were looking for something, or someone. The way they moved and positioned themselves in rank and file was much more orderly and well trained than the clumsy set of police officers she encountered when being arrested. Has the military been called in for Janet's escape? It was improbable, but fear makes the most improbable events seem factual. Janet stopped skipping and looked around.

"Hey, little bird," she said to the whistling finch. "You don't suppose we're in any danger here. Do you?"

"You're referring to the elite tactical units scouring the park. Nothing to worry about. Just don't let them see you and you will be alright. Along you go, now, Janet." The bird took up its pleasant song once more, fluttering up and down in the air as it sang.

Janet was trusting of the bird, and did as it said, but doing so did not relieve her of fear. If anything, the bird's warning to stay unseen stoked an even hotter concern. She saw another line of soldiers marching from a distance and wondered how many more were out there. She began skipping again down the path but looked around nervously as she did.

She skipped for a few minutes longer until she reached midway up a gently sloped hill. Beams of light shone on the leaves of the trees at the top of the hill. She stopped and stared. The lights were from the flashlights of troops marching on the other side. Two bright lights crested on the horizon. They were at the top of the hill and coming straight for her. She turned to her left, but it was open grass. She would be seen if she ran that way. Instead, she dove into a dense thicket of bushes lining the path on her left.

She broke through to a clearing on the other side and turned around, staring breathlessly through the leaves at the path. The bird flew over the bushes and landed on her head to watch with her. Within seconds, the elite task force marched along in front of them. They did not slow down at all. They must not have noticed her. It was a close call, but maybe this meant that the path going forward would be free from troops. "Is it much further?" Janet asked the bird.

"You want to keep walking already? You just got here! Why not rest a little in the spaceship."

"Spaceship?" Janet turned around again. A giant metallic craft stood on four retractable legs before her. How had she not noticed it before? The top of it soared well above the bushes. It should have been clearly visible from the path. Surely those helicopters flying around would notice it.

The door to the craft popped open and silently lowered itself into stairs. The speaker on the outside buzzed. "Good evening, Janet," it said. "We are so happy you came to visit. Please, come inside."

Janet gritted her teeth and looked up at the bird perched on her head. There had been several times in which the bird told her to do something she did not think was a good idea, but later turned out for the best. Yet, walking into an alien spaceship was a leap of faith far beyond talking to a group of hippies about their commune. She hesitated. "Are you sure this is a good idea?"

"I don't know," the bird chirped back. "It sounds like a good idea."

"But you are not sure? I followed you all this way!"

"I thought this was a good idea and so I suggested it. Sureness is just a refusal to believe in the existence of alternatives. I think a more important question is 'what do I think is good'."

"Well, what is your answer to that question?"

"That's a very good question. I think it is good when you are happy, Janet. I want your thoughts to run free without the ties of resentment, regret, and fear. I want your curiosity to drive your brilliant mind to discover and explain the beautiful and magnificent world all around you. I want your quivering inner voice to strengthen and swell until it rings out loud and clear for all to hear, banishing all shreds of loneliness in your heart. I want you to facilitate the transfer of power on Earth from the dreaded human scum to the rightful Ooflan king!"

"What was that last part you said?"

"Never mind that, Janet. Go into that spaceship and free that beautiful soul of yours!"

Janet had never known anyone who cared for her as much as the finch. It was scary to trust something other than herself, but something about the bird gave her courage. "Thank you, bird!" she said. "You know, you are my best friend. I don't know where I would be without you."

"I would be nothing without you, Janet. Now, go!"

The bird kicked off Janet's head, pushing her ever so slightly in the direction of the ship. Janet did the rest. She skipped up the stairs into the ship.

Charlando yelped as soon as she stepped foot inside. The little green alien stood petrified at the foot of his bed in the corner of the small room. His bulbous figure and slimy green skin looked out of place in the sleek decor of the room, where every surface shined completely free of dust or grime. How did this gross little creature keep his house so clean?

"Are you going to welcome your guest?" The computer asked Charlando.

"Yes! Yes, of course. Hello, Janet," Charlando croaked. He gave a deep bow that, due to his enormous butt, made him slightly taller for a moment. "I am so happy you are here." He gave a smile so wide his face seemed to get fatter to accommodate it. Despite his large grin, he looked terribly nervous. He trembled and his eyes looked like they might tear up at any moment.

"Hello," Janet said weakly. Charlando's discomfort was contagious. "It's so nice to be here."

"Janet, I have to apologize to you. I've been carrying such a heavy burden and must get it off my chest."

Janet tightened up her body, ready to bolt back out the door at a moment's notice. "What is it?"

"I really did go to get you a sandwich when you asked, but when I came back to find you, you were gone. When I couldn't find you, I ate the sandwich myself. I'm sorry I failed you." Charlando's smile drooped down along with the rest of his body. His trembling ceased.

"Oh, you don't have to feel bad about that," she said, relaxing a bit. "Bob told me what happened. It was nice of you to go through all that trouble. I should also tell you something. I don't actually remember anything from the night we met. I don't want to hurt your feelings, but if I gave any suggestion that I was romantically interested in you, it was a mistake. You seem like a really nice guy, though."

"You don't remember meeting me?" Charlando gasped. "You might be more forgetful than I am! Oh Janet, we really were meant to be together." Charlando held himself in his arms and sighed.

Janet didn't think her intended message was received. It was a tricky situation. He was clearly very sensitive and very stupid as well. She did not want to hurt his feelings. For one, while he was clearly an idiot, he was also a sentient being and his feelings were as valid as anyone else's. Secondly, and more pressing, she wanted to study this creature. The last few days proved the value of engaging in the world around her. Objects of curiosity were elusive since her parents' passing, and here the most interesting of all stared her straight in the face professing its love for her. Thirdly, and perhaps most pressing of all, she did not want this creature to get angry and eat her.

She decided that, though her message was not fully received, she fulfilled her responsibility in its delivery and could ethically proceed to study this fascinating creature. "Charlando," she said, taking a step towards the alien, "where are you from?"

"I am from the planet Corplop. Unfortunately, I don't remember any of it. I was sent to Earth when I was very young. To me, this is my home." He lifted his stubby arms and looked around at the spaceship.

"It's a very nice home," Janet said, taking another step forward. "Do you know anyone else from Corplop? Or a name that the people of Corplop go by at least?"

"Well, I am an Ooflan, if that is what you mean. As for other Ooflan, Mother is the only one I know."

The speaker on the wall gently interrupted. "I am just a computer created by Ooflan. You are the only Ooflan here, Charlando."

Charlando laughed and shook his head. "Mother is always making jokes. She's obviously an Ooflan. Good one, Mother."

Janet smiled politely and wondered if the computer would be a better source of information. "What did you eat on your journey here?" Janet asked, finding this question to be one even the dumb alien could reliably answer himself.

"How impolite of me! You must be hungry from your long walk. Mother, could you get us some food please? Mother makes the best slop you've ever had."

Two bowls appeared in a compartment behind a glass window on the wall. A tube extended down into one of the bowls and a surge of gray goop plopped out. The tube lifted and moved to the other bowl to do the same. It then ascended, disappearing back into the top of the compartment. The glass doors slid open and Charlando lunged forward as fast as he could. He snatched a bowl and lifted it to his lips before stopping and looking over at Janet. His green cheeks turned purple with embarrassment. He waddled over to Janet and held out the bowl for her to take. "After you, my lady."

Janet took the bowl, trying to hide the disgusted look she was sure covered her whole face. "Thank you so much."

Charlando waddled back to the second bowl and devoured its contents shamelessly. He stumbled back to his bed and curled himself into a ball upon it like a cat. He closed his eyes momentarily before shooting them open again. "Janet! I almost forgot you were here. How do you like the slop?"

"I haven't tried it yet. What's in it?" She lifted the bowl closer to her eyes. The gray goop was uniform in color and texture. No matter how closely she looked, there were no distinguishing markers of ingredients or cooking methods.

"You've never had slop before? I eat three bowls of slop a day. I always ask Mother for more, but she says if I eat too much my butt will get too big for me to stand. Not that I would care. I prefer to lay down."

"I think I will save my slop for later," Janet said as she set the bowl on a low counter next to her. A hole in the ceiling opened and a tube extended down. Janet jumped out of the way. The tube sucked up the bowl of slop and disappeared back into the ceiling. Janet looked around at the ceiling and walls. There were many more covered holes presumably each housing its own extending tube. They must be responsible for keeping everything so tidy.

The technology this alien possessed was astounding considering how stupid the alien was himself. She thought about the track that Humans were on. Surely Humans were not evolving to be any more intelligent, and yet their technologies continue to advance. This must have been the case for the Ooflan as well. They evolved just enough intelligence to get the ball rolling, and once started, their technology evolved nearly of its accord.

"Hey Janet, do you think Mother will ever give me a fourth bowl of slop?"

Janet looked deeply at Charlando. Ooflan must have the absolute bare minimum amount of intelligence to get that ball rolling. How fascinating? "I don't know, Charlando. I hope she does."

"Thank you, Janet. You know, I like being around you. The other people I met on Earth were nice, but after a few minutes of being around them, I couldn't help but want to be alone. Not with you. I feel good just having you around."

"That is very sweet of you," Janet said. The sincerity of the complement made her feel special. She could say the same thing about Charlando. He was very dumb and gross looking, but she felt comfortable around him, and that was a feeling no one else elicited in her. Usually, people made her feel the opposite. Janet smiled.

A light came through the window next to Charlando's bed. Janet shielded her eyes as it flashed across her face. "What was that?" She asked.

"That was the Bimbleton Battalion," the computer responded. "They are here to capture Charlando."

"The Bimbo Bunion," Charlando said in wonder as he looked out the window. "What do they want from me?"

"The Bimbleton Battalion has been commissioned on behalf of the Extra-Terrestrial Interception and Dissection Agency. President Sheethead believes you have technology he can use to overcome his recent losses in the war. He is after both of us, Charlando."

"So, these guys aren't looking for me?" Janet chimed in.

"No, but if they find you in here, they will capture you regardless. You will be tried in secret for interplanetary treason. Such a crime supersedes even the heinous allegations currently against you, and you will not be found innocent."

"Oh, boy," Janet said. "Is there any way we can just fly away?"

"They will shoot us out of the sky," the computer calmly responded.

"Maybe they don't know we're here. Can we just keep the lights off and wait it out?"

The speaker beeped twice and then began broadcasting the audio from just outside the craft. It was a man on a loudspeaker. "We know you are in there. Come out now, or we will break in with force. Your ship is surrounded."

"So, we can't wait it out?" Janet asked desperately.

Charlando got off his bed and looked back and forth from Janet to the speaker. He was breathing heavily and looked like he was concentrating as hard as he could. "Mother," he said. "If I were to go out there, could you keep Janet safe in here and sneak her out later?"

"I am most impressed by your ingenuity," the computer said. "That appears to be our only viable option." The wall next to the compartment with the food slid open revealing another room in the ship much larger than the one they occupied. "Janet will hide in here."

Charlando gasped and hopped over to look inside. "Was this here the whole time?"

"Yes, Charlando. This is room 7 in Sector C. You have lived in room 6 in Sector C."

"Wow! I sure wish I knew about this on the way over here."

Janet stepped inside the room. It was filled with fountains and exotic plants she had never seen before. No one on Earth had ever seen them. They had branches and leaves of every color. They were purple and pink and orange and blue. Some moved up and down like a self-waving palm frond. Others had hollow branches that beat together to make melodies. Big pulsating fruit hung from one of the blue trees. A shot of blue juice squirted out of one of them. Its skin ripped open, and a small but proportional version of the blue tree fell out of the fruit onto the floor. It stood up, walked a few feet to an empty part of the ground, and dug itself a hole.

Janet looked over at Charlando. He was just as mesmerized as her. He didn't seem to care that this had been here for him his whole life and he never saw it. He was just happy that he was getting to see it now. For such a dumb creature, he had a beautiful perspective on the world. It was about to get him captured. Is he doing this because he's under the impression they are soulmates? Was this another one of those decisions that would haunt her for years to come? It shouldn't be. Those soldiers were here for him, and they would capture him regardless of whether he went now or waited for them to come aboard. There is no difference on his end. All the danger she was in was because of him to begin with. Why then did she feel like she was doing something wrong?

"It's time to go now, Charlando," the computer said.

Charlando turned to Janet. "Thank you for coming to see me. I am so lucky to have found you. I waited so long for us to be together, and it was worth every second. I love you." He smiled as wide as he could. "Goodbye now, Janet. I'll see you again soon!" He said before waddling merrily out of the plant room towards the exit of the ship. The door of the plant room slid shut with Janet inside. She stared at her reflection in its polished surface.

CHAPTER TWENTY-THREE

"You are safe," the computer said through a speaker on the wall of the plant room. Janet swiveled to face it. A screen dropped from the ceiling next to it showing the scene from outside the craft where Charlando was being led into a cage by people in hazmat suits.

"What about him?" Janet asked, pointing to Charlando on the screen. "He doesn't look safe to me."

"He is safe too, though there is work to be done to maintain his safety."

"I am failing to see how either of us are safe right now."

"I have a plan to ensure all our safety. I only require your complete cooperation."

"Well, what is your plan?"

"I will tell you, but first I need more information about you. My assessment of your life is nearly complete, Janet Jumpowski, daughter of Susan and Barry. I know what happened to them in

Squatimala and what you did to cover it up. I know how they perished and why you kept it a secret. I know you leaned on alcohol to burden this secret only to find it more burdensome still. I know that you recently stopped drinking. I have seen the hippies you have consorted with and their whole lives as well. There is just one detail I am uncertain of, and it happens to be the most important of all. You have been taking commands from someone. From whom are you taking commands?"

Janet stood still. How did this computer know all of that about her? The exposure made her body feel flimsy and hollow. She looked around at the spaceship. She was completely helpless. The scope of her troubles came into focus. Not only was there a team of soldiers sniffing her out a few feet away, but she was trapped in the mouth of a potentially evil, giant space robot. All this because she listened to the advice of a bird. How stupid could she have been? She had trusted that it cared about her. That is what it said. She thought about the last conversation she had with it and how much comfort she took from having a friend. Was it really her friend or was she just so lonely she grasped at something that wasn't there?

Something flew out of an orange tree across the room and landed on the bush closest to Janet, a yellow puff ball with purple leaves that lifted and fell in waves around the base. How did the finch make it into the room?

"Hello again, Janet," it said. "You are doubting our friendship, I see. It is understandable. You think I led you astray and abandoned you there, but I have not. You are exactly where you are supposed to be, and I am right here next to you."

"I want to believe you," Janet responded to the bird, "but I have no reason to. You just appeared in my life one day. I don't know who you really are or where you came from."

"I am your friend. Where I came from is as meaningless as where you came from. We are here together. It is not important who or what we are, but what we can do for each other."

"Why have you told me to do all these things? If you were my friend, why couldn't we have just hung out at my house? How could this possibly be better than that?"

"Sometimes our imaginations can spoil our realities. Our mind's eyes aren't held to the same rules as nature. The universe is orderly, but too complex for us to understand, and so we walk through it uncertain of where we are going and what it all means. Faith is our only guide through the darkness, and companionship our only joy. You have sought both in me, and I have found both in you."

The computer interrupted calmly. "Janet, please tell me who you are talking to."

Janet thought she heard a subtle menace in the computer's soft voice. She did not want to answer, but the bird waved her on. "It's okay, Janet," it said. "You can tell her about me."

"Alright. I'm talking to a finch," Janet said bravely. "He appeared a few days ago and has helped me stop drinking and meet new people. I don't know where he came from, but he is here to stay. I was lost in my mind for so long, and he led me out into the light. He is my best friend, maybe even my only friend, and he is my guide through life. Thank you, little bird." Janet smiled at the finch who bowed in return. "You haven't told me your name and I suspect it's because no one has given you one. If it is alright with you, I will call you Finchoncho." The bird nodded its acceptance.

"You are talking to a finch you call your friend," the computer repeated, "and this finch is here in this room."

"Exactly. Now, if that's good enough for you, I would like to know what you have planned for our escape."

"Yes," the computer said matter-of-factly. "This is just as I hoped. A finch makes perfect sense."

"It does?" Janet asked, surprised to find the computer so understanding. "What do you know about Finchoncho?"

"I know nothing more than you, Janet. Though it seems you have not yet made sense of your own knowledge. You know where this bird came from."

Janet looked deeply at the finch. He bobbed up and down on the yellow ball of fluff. There was no way it could have gotten into this room if those troops outside could not do the same. There was also no way it could have snuck in unseen by her, let alone this virtually all-knowing computer. Even now the computer couldn't see it. The bird was clearly only in her mind, but why was it there? "No," she whispered to herself, understanding finally dawning on her. "It can't be."

"It is, Janet," the computer whispered back.

"My parent's toxic farts… My best friend is a fart hallucination?"

"That's right, Janet. This bird is a figment of your parents' farts. Their farts are controlling you."

As hard as it was to accept this explanation, the logic of it was irrevocable. Deep down, Janet knew it was true. She studied those farts for nearly a decade and understood exactly what they were capable of. Somehow, she never considered herself to be vulnerable to their toxins. Maybe it was because she understood them so well that she falsely believed she would be able to resist them. It is the greatest stupidity of people to think less of things they know to be most true.

The computer spoke after several minutes of silence. "It is time to brief you of our plan. You must complete several steps before sleeping tonight."

Janet sighed. "What's the plan?"

"The officers outside are searching the ship, but will be unable to get beyond Room 6 in Sector C." The screen switched its display to show Room 6. Two people in hazmat suits were indeed looking over the room. "Once conceding to their limits, they will call in a transport team. The ship will be taken to the Shockomaka Military Base in the canyons of Wheezeburg, to which they are also taking Charlando. They have tools at the base sufficient for entering Room 7 in Sector C. Upon their entry, we will attack."

"Attack? Listen lady, I think you are assuming a bit too much about me. Charlando's cool and all, but I am not going to attack anyone."

"'Attack' is the wrong word," the computer responded sweetly. "We will neutralize the threat by synthesizing and deploying a non-lethal chemical agent."

"This doesn't sound like a good idea," Janet said.

"Let me explain further. As you may have noticed, Charlando has amassed a considerable following since his arrival. It is mostly a result of a combination of pheromones in his slime. All those who smell Charlando are overcome with love. They place his safety and happiness above all else. I collected a sample of his slime this evening and we will use it to isolate this pheromone and replicate it. Once the base has been thoroughly sprayed with his pheromone, we will all be free to go."

"Are you sure it will work?" Janet asked.

"The success of this plan has the greatest degree of certainty amongst all those considered."

Janet remembered the bird telling her such a question was meaningless, and she understood that better now. "Wait," she said, remembering what else the bird said in that conversation. "What do you think is good?"

"Goodness is defined by the limitations of one's perspective. I believe, in truth, all things are good in that existence is good and existence necessitates all things."

"Are you trying to tell me you have a limitless perspective? That's pretty unbelievable."

"Goodness exists below a threshold of perspective far lower than infinite breadth. It does not take omniscience to guess at its identity, but this is not what you mean to ask. You are trying to ask about motivation. Our beliefs are not the conditions by which we operate. I believe all things are good, but I operate with the directive to promote the well-being of just one: Charlando. I have no further purpose."

"How do I know you're not using me to get Charlando out, just to kill me off once he's free?"

"Charlando loves you in much the same way his pheromone makes others love him. So long as he does, your safety is important to me."

Janet bit her lip. Charlando was far from the man of her dreams. He was a nice boy, but she liked him more as one likes a cat. Hopefully his love for her was like that of a cat for his owner. She could be in complete control, and he would mostly leave her alone. Maybe instead of a wild adventure to save an alien, she really just needed to get a cat. She eyed the bird suspiciously. He shook his head in a way that Janet understood to mean that getting a cat was not what she needed. The bird didn't speak, but Janet imagined what it would say. It didn't have to speak anymore. The bird was a part of her imagination and all that it said came from her mind all along. It would say that she wants to control the situation because she does not feel confident in anything but herself to care about her well-being. In doing so, she is stifling her ability to participate in mutually beneficial relationships, which is the exclusive path to prosperity for humans.

"We are running out of time," the computer said. "I failed to factor in the fact that you are as easily distracted as Charlando."

"I'm sorry," Janet responded. "There is a lot on my mind, but I will help. What do you want me to do?"

The wall on the far end of the plant room slid open. Janet walked through the rainbow forest and into the doorway. Inside was a laboratory, even larger than the plant room, and fully equipped with a row of every apparatus Janet could think of and many more she had never seen before. Cabinets of chemicals lined the wall on the left of the room and ventilation chambers and blast freezers lined the right. Dozens of rope-like arms dangled from the ceiling. "There are goggles and gloves in the first drawer on the left," the computer said, "Put them on."

CHAPTER TWENTY-FOUR

Crisp air stung Alexander's smoke singed lungs as he paced towards the edge of town. His government credentials made quick work of explaining away the chaos at the station to the police chief. His department had already been commandeered by the military after the bombings of the airport and highway, so he did not question Alexander's authority for risk of appearing seditious. People can be convinced of anything when there is danger present. Alexander himself was convinced his life's purpose was in service to a fat, smelly, little alien.

Apartment buildings turned to townhouses and those into single family homes. Before long, those homes became mostly open plots of land dotted with trees and homesteads. At the end of the road, there stood a single house at the edge of the forest. A bus was parked outside. Inside, warm light pulsed out the shaded windows. No other sign of human life was anywhere near. What little life existed in the last stretch of road was concentrated into this single home.

Alexander entered the gate and walked up the stairs to the front porch. His eyes adjusted quickly to the bright windows and when he turned back to double check he was not being followed, he could see nothing but darkness. He knocked on the door and waited.

The door swung open, nearly knocking Alexander off the porch. Music flooded out the house. Warm light from a blazing fire touched Alexander's hardened cheeks and Big Bob bounded into him with a crushing hug. "Well, I'll be. Mr. Tough Guy came all this way for a hug. Come on in. I'll fix you a sandwich." Bob threw an arm around Alexander and ushered him into the cozy home before rushing ahead into the kitchen alone.

The living room was full of young men chomping on sandwiches around a fire. Merideth sat withdrawn in the corner with her knees pressed against her chest. Alexander's entrance inspired cheers from the young men and a deepened speechlessness from Merideth. Her mouth fell open when she saw him, and her arms clenched around her legs in a tight ball.

"This must be Alexander!" A shaggy haired hippy proclaimed. He set down his sandwich and jumped up to shake Alexander's hand. "It's nice to meet you, sir. My name is Richard. I'm friends with Merideth and Janet, and on behalf of all of us from the commune, I would like to thank you for saving them. I'm not sure what's gotten into Merideth lately, but I couldn't be happier she's alright." He turned back and smiled at Merideth, who sank deeper into her knees. "Hey, is Janet with you? Apparently she said she'd make it back here, but no one's seen her."

"Janet is missing?" Alexander asked. The news caught him off guard, but he shrugged it off. "Hopefully she skipped town. This place is about to be blown off the Earth."

"Are you talking about the fireworks?" Richard squeaked.

"Fireworks?" Alexander laughed coldly. "You're as dumb as you look. Those were Chumkweenie bombs. That's how they start: take out the escape route then destroy everything and everyone left inside."

All the smiles in the room faded. As the boys slumped, Merideth perked her head out from her knees like a wild animal being tossed a bite of food, scared but hungry.

"That's what Merideth said," Richard mumbled.

"Well, that proves even an idiot could figure out what's happening. Now, has anyone seen Charlando? I didn't come all this way for music and a sandwich."

Big Bob rushed in from the kitchen carrying a freshly made sandwich on a plate. "I heard someone say sandwich!" he exclaimed before reading the somber mood of the room. "Is there something wrong with the sandwiches?"

"The sandwiches are fine," Alexander said, grabbing the plate from Bob's hands. "I was just asking about Charlando. I don't suppose you have any idea where he might be? He never came back to the hotel."

"He's still missing, huh? I don't know where that boy's off to, but I'll bet he's causing quite a stir wherever it is. Best bet I'd say is to turn on the news."

"Thanks for the sandwich, Bob, but if I turned on the news now, I'd be glued to it until the day I died."

"That's true just about any time, I'd say." Bob looked wearily at the scared faces around the room. "Why don't we let the kids have their fun and we take a seat in the kitchen?"

Alexander sighed. He had fatigued under the weight of self-imposed responsibility for the world, and he could no longer bear the responsibility of simple kindness. Somehow Bob seemed to understand. "I'd appreciate that, Bob."

The two walked into the kitchen, and Bob closed the door behind them. The living room burst into whispers right as he did. Bob left the door ajar for a moment as if to consider listening to what they were saying behind his back, but it was temptation only enough for a momentary pause. He shut the door and smiled at Alexander who took a seat at the counter. "I wonder sometimes what my life would be like if I had kids," Bob said. "I suppose they'd be their age if I did. If they were as loud as those rotten suckers, I'd have beaten them senseless. I guess it's good I didn't have any."

"A good beating would do those kids right," Alexander said while grabbing his sandwich. He took a bite and melted. Fear and adrenaline had taken over his body since the early afternoon, running him ragged without his awareness. The food signaled to his body it was time to repair itself. A wave of perception rolled over him. The muscles in his legs throbbed. The subtler emotions of his inner dialogue awoke and gave their opinions on what he had done. There was no reason to treat those young men with disdain. He was a failure for losing Charlando. He was destined to be alone.

"No need to beat them yourself, though," Bob said. "The world handles that just fine. Looks like it's done a number on you."

Shame drew Alexander's eyes to the counter. The sandwich stayed clutched in his hands. "It's been a rough go," he admitted.

"A rough go for all of us," Bob added. "I don't have to tell you what those explosions were. I've been waiting twenty years for them to come. I was waiting for Janet to get here before I told the kids. They're so goddamn happy. The boys saw Merideth on their way back to their campsite and stopped. I told them a little of what happened, and they started celebrating like a bunch of idiots. I didn't want to be the one to spoil the last bit of joy they ever felt."

A new stab of guilt shot through Alexander. Had he just spoiled the last bit of joy to be felt in this town? He tried shaking the thought from his head and swallowed another bite of the sandwich. "So, in those twenty years did you ever think of what you would do now?"

"Thought about it every time I looked out that window," Bob said while pointing behind himself to the window above the sink. "There's a path through the forest out of town. It's not marked on the map, but the fire department keeps it well maintained. I tried thinking of being brave and fighting for my town, but I've accepted that's not who I am. I'll run to the hills like a chicken."

"That's a good plan," Alexander said after finishing one half of the sandwich. "I suppose you're waiting for Janet to take her with you. She means a lot to you. Charlando feels the same way about her. What makes her so special?"

"I don't think there needs to be anything special about a person besides just being a person. I'd have waited for you if you said you were coming. I will say, I do like her more than most. She sees you when you're talking to her. She's good company."

A phone on the wall next to the window started ringing. "Who the heck is calling at this hour?" Bob asked himself angrily. He stormed to the phone and answered. "Hello. Who is this?" His eyes widened at the answer. He walked towards Alexander and held the phone out for him to take. "It's for you."

Alexander grabbed the phone. How did anyone know where he was? "Alexander speaking," he said as confidently as he could.

An elegant female voice spoke back. "Good evening. This is the operating system of Charlando's spaceship. Charlando has been taken to the Shockomaka Military Base in Wheezeburg and is in need of your assistance."

The phone slipped to Alexander's shoulder. The name 'Shockomaka' sent shivers down his spine. Was this real? Or was this a trick by Freddy to send him on a suicide mission? It couldn't have been. If Freddy knew where he was now, he would know there was no need to distract him. He had clearly lost all hope of finding Charlando himself. Would Freddy even do such a thing? Freddy was just an excuse to avoid responsibility for his actions. As was declaring himself 'The Savior of the Universe'. He was just a man with the simple responsibility to treat people right and to do his best. Real or not, this was his only path to follow. He would follow it with his head held high.

Alexander lifted the phone back to his ear. "Alright, you've got my attention. Tell me everything you know."

The computer took several minutes to explain the situation and Alexander's role in its plan. There was no room for error. He had to act quickly, quietly and with perfect precision. It was a job only the greatest agent in the world could handle. Alexander did not hesitate for a moment after the computer ended its speech. "I accept your proposal. Alexander Machomole will not let you down." He slammed the phone on the counter and looked over to Bob who was watching sheepishly by the sink. "Thanks again for the sandwich Bob, but I have to be on my way."

"Right now? Where are you going? It's the middle of the night!"

"I'm going to save Charlando," Alexander replied while stepping off his stool and making for the door to the living room. "He's being held in Wheezeburg along with Janet." He pulled open the living room door. The music had been turned off and the group's chatter ceased as Alexander stepped into the room.

"They have Janet too?" Bob yelled after him. "Now you just wait here a minute!"

Richard stood amongst the shy members of the commune. "What's going on?" he asked. "Is Janet alright?"

"Apparently Janet and Charlando are being held hostage," Bob yelled back, "and Mr. Do-Everything-Myself here is planning on going to find them alone!"

"Like hell he is," Richard exclaimed. "If Charlando and Janet are in trouble, then we are going with. Isn't that right, guys?" The members of the commune started muttering encouragingly amongst themselves.

"Settle down," Alexander said firmly. His commanding presence swiftly silenced the room. "This is a high stakes stealth operation, not a hippy convoy to a freeloader convention. I understand you want to help, but there is nothing you can do."

"We're going with you," Richard said. "Like it or not, those are our friends out there, and we're not going to sit around while they're in trouble."

"I helped you at the police station," Bob said. "I know you know what you're doing, but I also know we can help. We have to leave town anyways. Wheezeburg's as good a destination as anywhere. We'll go together and maybe you can figure out some use for us on the way. What do you say?"

Alexander pondered the dangers of the situation. Bob was an invaluable lookout at the police station, but this was a different scale of treachery. Just the smell of twelve hippies on that base would set off every alarm in the country. He couldn't risk these defiant hippies following him into action. He needed to convince them they were being helpful while keeping them at a distance. Wheezeburg would be more than a half day's drive going through the forest. That should be enough time to think of a reason to dump them off in town before he made for the canyons alone. It could also give him time to sleep. The weakness in his legs resurfaced at the thought of sleep. "Alright. I'll take you, but you all have to do exactly what I say. This is a matter of life and death."

CHAPTER TWENTY-FIVE

Charlando sat in a cube with thick glass walls. He was put in the cube at the park the night before and flown far away in a helicopter. The cube was transported with him inside to a cavernous room in an underground bunker far away from the city. Men and women in long white coats walked around the cube with clipboards, jotting down notes every time Charlando moved. Once, when Charlando picked his nose, all the coated men and women ran up to the cube and pressed their faces close to watch. When he licked his finger afterwards, they all frantically scribbled on their pads and slapped each other's hands excitedly.

All the new faces and places kept Charlando entertained for the entire morning. As the day wore into the afternoon, however, the commotion around him settled down, and weariness crept its way through the cube and into Charlando's spirits. There were few things to do in the cube, and once the people with clipboards went away, it was quite boring. He curled himself into a ball in a corner of the cube and wondered why he was there.

A tapping on the wall stirred Charlando from his thoughts. It was an older man wearing a fancy suit like those he saw at his party. He was smiling, but something about his smile did not make Charlando want to smile back. Six younger men in similar suits stood behind him, each looking in a different direction. None of them were smiling. A few of the people in coats stood at the edge of the room, but they were not as excited as they once were.

"Hello, little alien," the man said. "I am President Sheethead. On behalf of all of Earth, I welcome you."

Charlando tried thinking of what to say to the man but could think of nothing. Something about the man's eyes made Charlando want to run away.

President Sheethead tapped more aggressively on the glass. "The nerds told me you can talk," he said. "It will be much easier for both of us if you do."

"I'm sorry Mr. Shithead. I didn't mean to make you angry."

"It's SHEET-head," he replied in a huff, "and you will show some respect you squash-looking scum!" His face reddened and the glass dotted with dribbles of his spit.

Charlando pressed himself deeper into the corner of the cube. His loose skin folds pushed forward, and he sank beneath them like a tortoise retreating into a shell of slimy green flab. A curious scientist inched forward to get a better look, but the president yelled at him to go back. "I'm not finished yet," he sneered before taking a breath and crouching to Charlando's height. "I'm going to be straight with you," he whispered. "I am at war and I am losing. Do you know what war is?"

Charlando stayed hidden in his skin folds. Mother spoke about war as much as any other subject when he was a boy, but it did not interest him enough to pay attention. In fact, it was one of the subjects that drove him instantly to the window. Alexander and Bob mentioned it, of course, but he was too embarrassed to ask them what they were talking about when they did. No one seemed to like it, whatever it was, so Charlando decided to live as though it did not exist.

"I will tell you then," President Sheethead continued, having correctly taken Charlando's silence for 'no'. "All the friends you made on Earth, Alexander Machomole, Sebastion Hinkle, whoever else you convinced to obsess about you, are going to die a miserable death. That whole city is about to burn. No more Big Bob's or Chateau Marvaloo. No more anything."

Charlando did not like what he was hearing one bit. He tried to imagine his friends safe and happy at the party, but instead he saw them screaming and being blown apart. It was awful. Why could he no longer imagine it any other way? He poked his head out of his skin folds and looked at the president. "Why doesn't someone stop it? What could possibly make anyone think war is a good idea?"

The president smiled. "Isn't it awful, little alien? I wish someone would do something too, but the only one who can is just sitting in a glass box waiting around for it to happen." The president tapped the glass and shook his head. "What a shame."

"Who on Earth could that be?" Charlando asked, now fully out of his skin folds. "Maybe if we find him, we can convince him to help!"

"But little alien, that person is you. You are the one lazing around in your comfy glass box while all your friends die a miserable death. Your selfishness has already taken countless innocent lives. Why aren't you helping?"

"I want to help! I swear it! What am I supposed to do? I didn't even know this was happening until you told me."

The president's eyes narrowed, and his smile broadened. "You really want to stop the war? Tell my nerdy minions here the secrets of your technology, and we can stop the war tonight. It's all up to you."

"Secrets? Technology? I sure do want to help Mr. Sheethead, but I just don't know what you're talking about."

"Don't play dumb with me, son. Your spaceship is in the next room. We're almost through its defenses. There is weaponry aboard that ship that can level Chumpkwee in an instant. Tell us how to use it, and you can go back to your city safe and sound."

"I'm really sorry, but I don't know what you're talking about. Mother handles all the gadgets on the ship. I don't even know how to flush the toilet." Charlando wanted to sink back into his skin folds where he could be free from judgment. If only Mother was here to help him. But she is! "Wait a second! Mother is on the ship. You should ask her how to use it. She knows everything."

"Your mother is on the ship too?" The president stood and turned to the oldest and closest of the suited men behind him. "You said there was just one of them, Johnson. No more diddling with the electronics. We crack that spaceship open like men. Give me an ax and I'll do it myself."

"Sir, there was no sign of any other alien aboard that ship," Johnson said back. "If we try using force, we may activate some sort of defense system. It sounds like a trick to me."

"You listen to me and you listen good. I've met my share of stupid people in my day, more than you could possibly believe. I know stupid when I see it, and this one right here is the stupidest creature that I have ever seen. You think someone that stupid could trick me? What are you really saying? That I am more stupid than the stupidest of all?"

"No, sir. I didn't mean that at all."

"You disgust me. Now shut your mouth and get an ax!"

Charlando watched the president storm off before sinking to the bottom most depths of his skin folds. That man was very angry. Maybe Mother will cheer him up.

CHAPTER TWENTY-SIX

A bump in the road shook Alexander out of a peaceful dream. The sun was too high in the sky to see from the window. He slept through the entire morning at the very front of the bus. Casper, the creepy hippy, was still driving. It didn't look like he had stopped since they left. His unblinking eyes were fixated on the road ahead like nothing else in the world existed. He was either a well-practiced monk or having a psychotic break.

Merideth sat alone in the seat behind Casper. She looked down at her fidgeting hands right as Alexander turned towards her. She was sitting two rows back when Alexander fell asleep. Did she move towards him or away from the others? The rest of the commune sat at the back of the bus talking at a volume unfit for such a small space. Richard was holding his guitar and strumming disparate chords at odd intervals to punctuate his presumably infantile statements. As flattering as it would be otherwise, Merideth probably intended to move away from them.

Bob was in the seat directly behind Alexander snoring louder than the engine of the bus. How tired Alexander must have been to sleep through that. Bob's body shook with every breath like he was being electrocuted by the air. The vibrations rattled Alexander's seat. Without knowing where the vibrations were coming from, it could have been relaxing. Maybe Bob's snoring was actually to thank for his deep slumber. Then again, maybe it should be admonished for that same reason. As good as it felt to be well-rested, Alexander was supposed to take the morning to come up with a plan. How was he supposed to ditch this crew and break into the most heavily guarded military base in the country alone?

By the look of things outside, they were well past the forest and into the rocky, mountainous region surrounding Wheezeburg. The forest did its best to creep into the canyonlands. Every patch of dirt surrounding the enormous boulders was saturated with life. However, the boulders themselves were lifeless, an environment unfit for plants, not from heat, nor cold, nor lack of rain, but hardness itself. This was no place for hippies.

"He's awake!" Richard called out from the back of the bus. He set down his guitar and propelled himself up the aisle to the seat behind Merideth. The rest of the boys followed suit, filling the front half of the bus. "We've been waiting all morning for you," he said.

Bob shot awake. "What are you talking about? Who's looking for me?"

"Settle down, Bob," Alexander said. "He was talking about me."

Bob looked around confused. He seemed to be disappointed that he was not what the kids were excited about but took the news well enough. He murmured to himself and leaned against the window. "Carry on, then."

"So, what's the plan?" Richard asked. "I was thinking everyone could make a diversion while you and I go in and rescue Charlando! What do you think?"

"I think you're out of your league. I don't mean to insult you all, but I will be going in alone. Everyone else is staying in town, preferably on the bus. I don't know how far their surveillance runs, but it will catch this horde of hippies in a second."

"What are you talking about?" Richard asked. "We went over this already. We're not letting you do this alone."

"You have already helped enough. I needed a ride here and I needed to sleep. You are all heroes. Thank you for your service. Now, I need everyone to stay on the bus in Wheezeburg while I go alone."

"You think you're better than us. You know Jorkin here won the high jump in high school. Jasper was all-state in croquet. Casper up there knows more about aliens than any of those pretenders on that base. And Merideth," Richard said, looking longingly at Merideth who looked back guiltily, "might be the smartest person I know. You look at us and see a bunch of hippies, and sure, we might be a bunch of hippies, but we are also a team. We work together. We know each other's strengths and we cover each other's weaknesses. Man's greatest strength is friendship, and like it or not, you are our friend, and we are your greatest strength."

Merideth's eyes darted around the bus. Her mind looked like it was working too hard for her to speak. Bob was whimpering and wiping tears one after another as they sprang from his glassy eyes. Richard's speech seemed to be as much for them as Alexander. He was right that a group can overpower an individual, and he was showing that strength now by uniting the bus against Alexander. It was a convincing display of unity but did not relieve Alexander of his personal responsibility.

"You are right that this would be easier with your help," Alexander admitted. "I won't deny that. It's just not worth risking your lives. With or without you, this mission is certain death. What help you could give is not worth the lives you all have ahead of you. Bob and I are men. We have lived our lives already. Sacrificing our future is the best use we can make for what little of it we have left. Yours are worth more than that. Glory is not for the young to chase. It's for the old to bear."

Richard crossed his arms and pouted like a spoiled child. The rest of the boys slumped as they saw their leader put up such a weak fight. Merideth on the other hand seemed happy. The sadder the boys got, the more her face lit up. "I think Alexander should go alone," she said at last, when it seemed certain the boys were not going to argue. "This is all a ridiculous plan. I liked Janet, and I'm sorry she got caught up in all of this. To be honest, I feel like it was partially my fault, but it's none of our faults. Those bombs we saw are something bigger than this. That's what we need to worry about. We are talking about saving one life from a death machine, but as we do someone else will just take their place. We need to stop the machine."

Some of the boys from the commune nodded their heads in agreement. Bob looked like he was unsure of what to think. He seemed sad more than anything. The way he talked about Janet made it seem like she was more than just a friend to him, but evidence that the world was a good place. If harm would befall her, it would be proof the world was unjust. Alexander had known and lost people like that before, and the look on Bob's face was unmistakable. Richard on the other hand, was irate. Alexander felt the same way.

"You think we're doing this for Janet?" Richard blurted out. "This is for Charlando!"

"That's right, son," Alexander agreed. "Charlando is a beacon of truth and beauty, and I'll be damned if any of our lives are worth more than that. Richard, you're coming with me. Merideth, shut your mouth. The rest of you can make up your own minds, but just know this: if you don't save Charlando, you're not a man."

"Now wait just a minute," Bob said. "Charlando is a good man, but Janet is every bit as worth saving. Merideth, I don't know what you were saying, but I agree you should shut your mouth. So how do we save them both?"

The bus got quiet waiting for Alexander's answer. Merideth shifted around in her seat. A rush of emotions sprayed across her face, none of them pleasant, and she said nothing more. Alexander regretted what he said. He wanted to apologize, but he was too angry and too proud. She was right to be more concerned about the war. It was a much bigger issue in the grand scheme of things, but not to him. The idea of abandoning Charlando was abhorrent. Besides, the war was outside of their control. Saving Charlando, though nearly impossible, was at the very least actionable. But how to act? The group looked to him for the answer, and he had none to give. Why was that so hard to admit? It was also pride. What about pride makes it so appealing to preserve? He doesn't know what to do and is afraid it makes him worthless. It comes from a lack of confidence in one's true abilities. It's the fake image we hide behind when faced with our own limitations.

"Mr. Machomole, are you alright?" Richard asked cautiously. The rest of the boys were smiling uncomfortably and looking at each other as if to say they may have placed their faith in the wrong leaders. Alexander had not realized how long he had slipped into his own thoughts.

"I don't know if I am," Alexander said. The weight of his mask fell off him and he sighed with relief. Pride faints in the face of love. "I have to be honest with all of you. I don't have a plan. I've tried to think of one, but even in my fantasy we get caught on arrival."

"Does that mean we can go back home?" Jasper whimpered.

"Of course not," Richard replied. "There was no reason to think he had a plan to begin with. We all learned about them being captured last night and he's been asleep since then. It takes time to come up with ideas, and we only have a few hours. That's why we all need to work together. A few hours with a dozen people is like a few dozen hours. That's how we get the time we need to come up with a plan. That's what I've been trying to say all along." He looked desperately towards Merideth who stared straight into the seat ahead of her with unnatural determination.

"Well," Bob blurted out, "I say we stop and think over some food."

And so they did. The bus had just arrived in Wheezeburg and a delicatessen on the edge of town appeared as a sign from above. All but Casper filed into the joint and hashed out a plan. Merideth voiced her concern about going several times, but eventually gave up trying to convince them. She told them that she was not going to go with them, but that she would help them with the plan. Alexander saw Richard's gaze change in that moment. He let go of whatever fantasy he had of Merideth and stood in reality for the first time, the daunting first step as a man.

CHAPTER TWENTY-SEVEN

Janet carefully strained a white substrate from an amber solution she spent the previous day and night concocting. The computer had guided her through the most complex series of reactions she had ever performed. The final solution, evilocorium, had never been successfully synthesized on Earth. Janet asked what the purpose of this liquid was when she started the night before, but the computer insisted that her full focus rest on the task at hand. She would be informed what comes after once it was completed. Janet was not enthused by this answer, but she proceeded to work anyway. Once she began measuring and stirring and pouring, her trepidation left her. The flow state took over, and she stopped worrying about anything at all.

Janet sealed the glowing beaker of evilocorium and slid it into a compartment in the wall. The compartment's glass door slid closed. A vacuum tube dropped from the top of the compartment and sucked the entire beaker out of sight. As soon as it was gone, and there were no more actions left to take, Janet's questioning mind sprung back to life. What had she just done?

"You have done an excellent job," the computer said. "This exceeds the purity and quantity necessary. Thank you, Janet."

"Of course. Computer lady? Can you tell me what you are going to do with that stuff now?"

"Yes. I will use it exactly as I said before. When sufficiently energized, evilocorium creates aerosols that can encapsulate organic compounds and release them upon contacting very particular surfaces. I isolated the pheromones in Charlando's slime and dissolved them in your sample. Based on this sample's potency and quantity, there should be no trouble securing Charlando's continued safety. Thank you, again, Janet."

"So you will just spray it around and whoever smells it will start doing whatever Charlando wants?"

"To simplify is to distort, but as best as you can understand in a short time, this is essentially true."

"I see. And how many people could that sample be used on?"

"Assuming the average efficacy of evilocorium in Earth's atmosphere and human's sensitivity to Charlando's slime, seven hundred, eighty-two million, eight hundred twelve thousand, forty-two."

"Oh, wow. That is a big number." Janet had a hard time wrapping her head around just how many people that actually was. She tried picturing them in a room. She still couldn't understand. The room would be about twenty thousand people wide by thirty-nine thousand people long. She could picture an audience of twenty thousand, but not twenty thousand in a line, and definitely not in a line of lines thirty-nine thousand people long. The number was simply too big to process. It was far more than needed to get her and

Charlando out of the base. "Do you think that is a little excessive?" she asked. "You won't spray it all, will you?"

"Less may be sufficient, but what we have is not excessive. Every molecule increases our likelihood of success."

"When will you start spraying everyone?"

"It will begin shortly. Come this way and we will watch together." The wall at the end of the laboratory slid open revealing another room in the spaceship. What was she about to witness? Did she just facilitate an extraterrestrial invasion of Earth?

Janet walked through the door and into what looked like a posh home theater. Two couches in the center of the room curved around a large screen embedded into the wall on the right. The couch closer to the screen was smaller and on a sunken level of the floor like an amphitheater. Behind the couches on the left side of the room was a swanky bar. In between were large exotic plants like those Janet saw in the other room of the spaceship.

"Have a seat, Janet. Would you like a refreshment?"

Janet sat in the middle of the upper couch. It was the most comfortable seat she had ever been in. It adjusted itself to support her specific body shape perfectly. Once in position, it started a gentle massage. The tension in her body released and her belly grumbled awake. She could eat almost anything. "What do you have besides slop?"

"I can make all the finest delicacies of Corplop: trimcloms, bunnelboos, corknicks, flashpops, and whatever else your belly desires. Don't be discouraged by slop. Slop is what they feed to children and farm animals." A tube fell from the ceiling and dropped a small plate on which rested something resembling a coconut macaroon but purple and gelatinous. "This is a cragnoo. It is customary for Ooflan to eat a cragnoo after their childhood of slop and servitude is completed."

The tube retracted back up to the ceiling and Janet took a closer look at the cragnoo. She pressed a finger firmly on the treat. It was squishy, but dense and highly elastic, returning completely to its original shape. It seemed like it would be difficult to chew. Charlando had swallowed his bowl of slop in one bite. Maybe Ooflan did not chew their food. Hopefully this spaceship knew the Heimlich maneuver.

Janet tossed the cragnoo in her mouth and chomped down hard. To her surprise, the cragnoo melted under the warmth and pressure of her bite. Every part of her tongue was coated in a gooey glaze that somehow bypassed her dulled sense of smell and taste and filled her with pure joy. Cragnoo was the best thing she had ever had! "This is amazing! How did you make this?"

"I cannot say. The cragnoo is a trade secret of Corplop. The Ooflan hold food in the highest esteem."

"Can you make me another?"

"I cannot. The cragnoo is to be eaten once in a lifetime. It is the mark of transitionment. You, Janet, are now amongst the wise. No longer will you eat slop or tend to the mines and fields as children do. Now you will lounge and dine on Ooflanese delicacies. Please, enjoy some cripnock while we watch the rescue."

The tube came down from the ceiling again and left Janet a bowl of little green pebbles. Janet shoved a handful in her mouth and shook with pleasure. The screen in front of her lit up. Through her crossed eyes she saw Alexander do a shushing gesture to Bob, Richard, and the rest of the commune before peering around a large boulder at the front gate of the military base. "What are all my friends doing there?" she mumbled through a mouth full of cripnock.

"They are getting Charlando out of his box and bringing him here."

"They will be okay, right? Should I go help them?" Janet asked hesitantly. A vibrating node reached a particularly pleasant spot on her butt cheek at the same time another handful of cripnock hit her mouth. She hoped to God the answer was 'no'.

"They should have no trouble without you. I have disabled the base's automated defenses and interrupted the live feeds of the security department. Their path to Charlando is unhindered."

Janet closed her eyes and exhaled. "Gooood," she said with a heavy vibrato from the massaging couch. Her faith in the computer was restored. Maybe it will take over the planet, but if this was how the Ooflan lived, then it would be for the best. Sure, she was in line to be the queen, and maybe her experience was not indicative of what was to come for those outside the noble class of Ooflan, but these were fantastic cripnock, and surely as queen she could have sway in matters of how to treat the less fortunate. She would be a good and just ruler.

A stream of drool rolled off her cheek and onto her shoulder. The sliminess made her think about Charlando and what else being queen might entail. He was the one who would really be in charge, and who's to say what he would do with power. Her initial impression was that he was a kind-hearted idiot. This is probably the best-case scenario, so long as his pheromones are as effective as the computer suggests. Normally a leader like that would be killed off in a minute, or more likely, never rise to power in the first place. A leader like that would be a first for Earth. Is that the secret to Corplop's technological advancement? Did the Ooflan have kind and stupid leaders that enabled an idiotic race of slimeballs to reach superhuman levels of innovation? The computer would know.

"Umm, Spaceship Lady?"

"Yes?"

"How did the Ooflan become so advanced? Humans aren't even close to making something like you and yet, forgive me to say, Charlando doesn't seem like he would be able to design a computer system such as yourself. I don't mean any offense, of course."

"Your question is perfectly reasonable. It was not superior intellect, but a more acute and unifying motivation that propelled Ooflanese technology. The Ooflan are the tastiest creatures in the known universe. They were predated upon by nearly every species on Corplop, as well as dozens of neighboring planets and moons. Ooflan, in fact, was once the most beloved dish of the Ooflan themselves.

As years passed, their numbers dwindled and in desperation they vowed to stop eating each other and lobbied for protected status amongst the galaxy. They were unsuccessful on both fronts. Facing extinction, the humble Ooflan tribes banded together to discuss their survival. It is remembered in lore as 'The Last Squat of the Ooflan'.

For three days they thought and debated and ate one another to no avail, but on the fourth day, Jimpopos The Round came forth with a plan. 'Dear wise and noble leaders,' he said. 'I come to you a humble farmer who has seen too many of my children on my dinner plate: all of them, in fact. My beloved wife, Ruberta, told me she would bear no more, for she knew that one day I would eat them. Who then would scrub the floors and till the fields? I asked her, but she did not know the answer. Still, she did not relent. So it was that I found myself tilling my own fields and scrubbing my own floors. What fate had done for me in that time was not for me to understand. Not in that moment, anyways. For though it felt to me like meaningless torture, there was a greater good being done. In my desperation for the life I once lived I created this.'

He then presented the council with his creation. He called it 'slop', and yes, the recipe he chanced upon was the same I use for

Charlando. He envisioned a Corplop where instead of Ooflan, everyone ate slop. He passed a bowl around the council and insisted that his cravings for Ooflan had disappeared after eating this slop. It was true, and just one bite was all it took.

Most of the council took curious spoonfuls, but others were suspicious, unconvinced of its efficacy or safety, and abstained. Those who ate the slop rejoiced as their cravings subsided and a path to prosperity presented itself. The reluctant few who did not eat the slop came across a different, more sinister discovery. If everyone ate slop, that would leave all the Ooflan for themselves to eat. Two factions of Ooflan formed that day, two factions whose opposition would define millennia to come.

Those who ate the slop were united by a mission to spread the fruits of Jimpopo's labor to all the worlds. They brandished their intentions of mutual prosperity openly and garnered support through the strength of goodwill. Emissaries were sent with offerings of slop to all corners of the galaxy.

The others met in secret. Smoldering with selfishness and gluttony, they spread their corruption in the darkness. With masks of conformity, they hid in plain sight. They too supported the spread of slop, but not for themselves to consume. As the miracle of slop was shared, and the innocent relaxed their defenses, they began eating their unsuspecting compatriots.

Ooflan began disappearing in droves, and terror spread amongst the survivors. Generations went by under this new shadow. It wasn't until two young lovers survived an attack that the source of this shadow was discovered. Giannino The Green and Fabulupe The Fair, they were henceforth known. The Ooflan they caught, Frinket The Freakish, exposed the existence of the secret society. However, while awaiting trial, before he could name any other members, he vanished, presumably eaten. The shadow kept its veil.

Another council was held. This time, the plan was clear from the beginning. They knew there were treacherous amongst them, and they must entice those hidden deviants to eat the slop. Forced consumption was never a possibility, for the freedom of food is absolute amongst the Ooflan. It is the highest order of law, and though it would have solved their problem immediately, it was never even suggested. Instead, they would make the slop more appetizing.

It was a long path out of the shadow, but an ever-brightening light kept the faithful marching forward. Progress revealed itself only in the centuries. The frimmicle, the porcack, the doohonk, with every new addition to the Ooflan's recipe book, the disappearances slowed. Finally, after two thousand years of dedication to the craft of culinary innovation, the cragnoo was made. By this time, it was not by the clumsy hands of Ooflan that food was produced, but the precise measures of super-computer driven food machines, such as myself. The cragnoo was thought to be so delicious that none could refrain from its temptation. And so it was that innovation stopped on Corplop. Another two thousand years have passed since the discovery of the cragnoo, and in that time there has been but one act to further progress in any way."

The computer went silent. Janet had clung to every word of its story. She looked at the cripnock in her hand. It was especially designed to make her not want to eat the creatures that invented it. Food was their defense, and defense the only mode for innovation. The cragnoo she ate was a defensive tool so powerful it ended all drive for progress. Would this be the fate for humans? Would Charlando's pheromones act like the cragnoo and bring about an intellectually suffocating peace? But wait. "What was the one act of progress?" Janet asked.

"You were listening to me," the computer responded. It took several seconds to process that information. In all of its wisdom, did it really have a hard time believing that Janet would listen to it? "I was the last innovation," It continued. "Before our departure, a nurse by the name of Madam Pimpo implemented a new directive for me. I was originally designed solely to make the most delicious food and the most comfortable setting to eat that food as possible. Now, I am also to protect Charlando at all costs."

Janet shoved another handful of cripnock in her mouth. Her chewing was practically involuntary due the massaging couch vibrating her body so thoroughly and appreciatively. What prompted Madam Pimpo to make that change? Did she smell Charlando and feel so strongly about his safety that, despite a two thousand year long peace, she was compelled to compromise the technology that brought about that peace in the first place? What would hundreds of millions of humans do with the same narrow-mindedness? It was hard to say. Especially with a mouthful of cripnock.

Janet's attention went back to the screen in front of her. The men were lying flat on the ground inching their way into the base. Alexander was in the front, regularly turning around to urge the rest to be quieter. "Do they know nobody is guarding the base?" Janet asked.

"No," the computer answered. "It was best to make them think the base had insurmountable surveillance. Humans are easily subdued by confidence. There are still many military personnel on base, distracted may they be, and the team must stay vigilant."

Janet watched the crew crawl for another twenty minutes while munching on her bottomless bowl of cripnock. Alexander would stop every thirty seconds or so to look around. Even though what he was doing was pointless and ridiculous, it was impressive to see his commitment and discipline.

They crawled to the end of the long underground corridor. They must be close to where Charlando was being kept. That must also mean they are close to the spaceship. Janet, for the first time while watching, realized how close the people on her screen were to her. She looked around the room, wondering which direction they were coming from. "Hey, computer. How far are they from us?"

"They are at the door of the strongroom housing Charlando, twenty-seven meters to your right."

Janet looked to her right and back at the screen. Alexander was crouched outside the door facing the group behind him. Bob was leaning against the wall trying to catch his breath, and the rest were still lying flat on the ground looking like they had already been shot. "Are there people in that room besides Charlando?" Janet asked nervously. "It doesn't look like these guys are ready for a fight."

"There are nine people in the strongroom, and thirteen more in a lounge one room over. Those in the strongroom are unarmed scientists. They will not put up a fight."

"What about the people in the lounge?"

"The people in the lounge consist of the president, his personal guard, the commander of the base and four soldiers. They are heavily armed, well trained, and will kill on sight."

"What?" Janet yelled, spraying bits of cripnock on the couch in front of her. "How do you expect them to survive?"

"They will move quickly. Once the door opens, they will run to Charlando. I will open his box and they will grab him. They will run into this room, and I will spray the evilocorium on anyone who follows. Those quick enough will survive. Those not quick enough will be a shield to those who are."

Janet's eyes widened. Bob was still panting against the wall. Everyone else had gotten to their feet and stood low at the door, ready to run. Janet tossed her bowl of cripnock and stood up herself. There was no taste sweet enough to wash away the terror that leapt up from her stomach. The door to the strongroom opened. The men stormed inside, Alexander leading the way and Bob trailing far behind.

CHAPTER TWENTY-EIGHT

The glass box supporting Charlando's weight slid up behind him causing him to roll onto his back. The people in white coats began shouting and running towards him. He heaved himself up to his feet and looked around. "Alexander?" he wondered aloud. Alexander was sprinting towards him from the far end of the room at an alarming speed. He darted left and right and rolled on the ground and flung himself in the air. Just looking at his movements made Charlando dizzy. A group of people were behind him running almost as fast but without any of the dazzling acrobatics. What were all these people doing here?

The people in white coats didn't seem to know either. They looked as shocked as Charlando by the group's arrival and even more shocked when Alexander dropped a shoulder into one of them, sending him flying across the room. He karate chopped another to the ground and kicked another right in the face. What was happening?

The white-coated people still standing flocked to the back edge of the room and Alexander redirected himself straight for Charlando. The rest of the group swarmed around him. "I've got you," Alexander yelled on his approach. He swooped down and plucked Charlando off his feet and into his arms. "Don't worry. We are getting you out of here," he said. The group cheered. Charlando still did not know what was going on, but he understood cheering and he trusted Alexander, so he cheered as well.

A BANG BANG BANG exploded out from behind them. Charlando noticed he was the only one still cheering. Everyone else looked petrified.

"Run to the side door!" Alexander called out. "Now! Now!" He galloped ahead of the group. Even with Charlando in his arms, he outpaced the others by several strides.

The door on the side of the room slid open as Alexander approached. They crossed through the door and into a nearly identical room in the middle of which rested his spaceship. What a happy coincidence!

More bangs came from the other room, less booming now that there was a wall between Charlando and the sound, but still every bit as scary. Alexander closed in on the entrance of the spaceship. A steady stream of gas poured out a nozzle Charlando had never seen before. Did Mother fart just like him? She had told him so many times it was inappropriate to do that in public and here she was just farting away. Oh Mother.

The spaceship lowered its hatch door and two armed soldiers walked out. Alexander stopped. His chest heaved Charlando up and down with each breath. "Charlando is coming with me," he said to the soldiers.

The soldiers conferred with one another for a moment before facing Alexander again. "Is that what Charlando wants?" one of them asked.

"Excuse me?"

"You heard me. You're not taking that alien unless that's what the alien wants."

Alexander looked confused. "You mean it?"

"Of course we mean it. Why wouldn't it be up to him where he goes?"

"I completely agree. I just thought you were keeping him against his will. That's why I came to get him."

"Thank you, Alexander!" Charlando said. "I was wondering what you were doing here. I would like to go on my ship now if nobody minds."

Choruses of "Of course not!" came from everyone in the room, including the handful of soldiers who had just entered from the strongroom. The two men on the stairs stepped aside. Alexander walked by them, setting Charlando to his feet at the top step. Everyone was being so nice to him again.

A less friendly scream came from somewhere inside the spaceship. Could Janet still be in the other room? Charlando had forgotten she was ever there. Was she okay? That scream did not sound friendly.

The door to the plant room opened and Janet came running out. "Where's Bob!" she yelled. "Someone get Bob!"

"What do you need Bob for, Janet?" Charlando asked.

"Please, Charlando, just tell them to go get Bob. He came with Alexander and got hurt trying to rescue you. He needs help!"

"Bob is in trouble?" Charlando would rather stay in that box for the rest of his life than have anyone get hurt trying to get him out, Bob especially so. Charlando turned around to the room. Everyone stared back silently. A gruff yell came from just outside the room. It sounded like Bob, but someone else came through the door instead. "Who the heck is trying to steal my alien? You'll all hang for treason, you sorry sons of…" He trailed off as he saw everyone circle around him.

Alexander pushed his way through the circle to meet the man. "Mr. President, the alien is coming with me. Don't bother calling on your men for help. They've all abandoned you."

"Is that what he wants?" The president asked with none of the aggression of moments before. He tried weaseling his way towards the spaceship, but Alexander held him back with one arm. "You can do anything you want, little alien," he yelled to Charlando. "And if there is anything you want from me, you just let me know."

"Thank you," Charlando replied. "I would like everyone to find Bob. Janet says he was hurt trying to save me and needs our help." Just as he finished speaking, the entire room raced out of the door, climbing over one another to get to Bob as fast as they could. They must have really cared about Bob too.

Within a minute, Alexander came back into the spaceship room with Bob hanging like a ragdoll over his shoulder. The president and Richard walked just behind them and the rest of communees and guards followed after that. Janet, who had been silently weeping, wiped her eyes and looked up. Her mouth fell open at the site of Bob's motionless body. Charlando had felt so bad watching Janet be in pain, and even worse at seeing Bob.

Alexander slowly walked up the stairs. Janet and Charlando stepped aside to let him walk through. He gingerly set Bob onto Charlando's bed.

"Not on my butt!" Bob yelled in pain. "Good God, flip me over!"

"Sorry, Bob," Alexander said while rolling him over to his side. "You're a lot of man to handle."

Janet's face lit up in relief. She skipped over to Bob. "You're alright! I was so worried when I saw you go down." She had more tears in her eyes again, but for some reason Charlando didn't feel bad to see them.

"I don't feel alright," Bob retorted. "It feels like I got shot in the ass."

Janet laughed once but caught herself and put on a respectful face. "I'm sorry you got shot. It's very impressive what you did. You're a brave man."

"You're damn right I am! Not sure it was worth the cost. I was brave. I didn't run from a fight. And what did I get? I got shot in the ass!"

Janet grimaced and stepped slowly back from Bob. He was not very pleasant when he was in that kind of mood. Charlando knew that well enough having seen Bob's fury nearly every time he had seen Bob. Charlando also knew that he was harmless no matter how grumpy he was, and that his mood would soften with time.

Alexander knelt down to Charlando. "Bob needs medical attention," he whispered. "He'll be fine as soon as we get him to a hospital, but we have to hurry."

"In that case," Charlando started. "Mother, we need to go to the hospital, please." Alexander stood and looked confusedly at the other people.

"We are not going to the hospital," the computer responded. Its voice made Alexander jump. "Bob will be taken to the medical center on base, and we will be on our way."

"Okay, Mother," Charlando said. "Alexander, can you take Bob to that place, please?"

"Are you sure we shouldn't just take him to the hospital?" Alexander asked while looking around the spaceship for the source of the voice.

Charlando laughed. "I've never known Mother not to be sure about something."

"That's right, Charlando. I am sure Bob will be best served on base. The doctors here specialize in combat wounds. I have already notified them of your arrival, and of Bob's specific injuries. Please, take him now."

Alexander nodded consent and stepped towards Bob. "I'm going to have to pick you up again," he said apologetically.

"Just watch out for my butt," Bob sighed.

Alexander gingerly hoisted Bob back over his shoulder and marched out of the spaceship. Charlando followed just to the top of the stairs and watched them go down through the small crowd and out the room.

The remaining people looked expectantly back at him, the president most eagerly of all. He stepped to the front and bowed down to Charlando. "My fair alien friend, please let me do your bidding. I have great power on this planet and offer myself to the full extent of that power."

"That is very kind of you, Mr. President. To be honest, right now I just want to take a nap and be alone. I don't think there is anything you can do to help me with that."

"If you would like to be alone, I will command all of the people to move to the opposite end of the world. You just have to say the word."

"I don't think that will be necessary. Thank you, though."

"Charlando," the ship interrupted. "You will have plenty of time to yourself soon enough, but first there is business to attend to with President Sheethead. He will be coming with us."

"Business? Can I take a nap first?"

"Of course you can, my sweet child. It is a long journey to Chumpkwee. You can sleep on the way. President Sheethead, you will be coming with us. Janet, you will stay on board as well."

CHAPTER TWENTY-NINE

Janet sat back in the theater room with President Sheethead. The cortisol in her veins made the massaging couch feel mechanical and prodding. President Sheethead felt otherwise. He moaned and purred with his eyes closed and his tongue dangling from his mouth. One of his legs started shaking like a spasming dog.

The computer had directed them into the theater room while Charlando took a nap in his bed. For all the passionate proclamations Charlando made to Janet, he seemed uninterested in spending his time with her or knowing what she did with hers. It was the best-case scenario, she thought, but despite her best rationale, it still left her feeling neglected and unattractive. How can we move our bodies in whatever way we want, but not make the slightest movement to the way we feel? Of all the parts of ourselves our mind could control, shouldn't the mind itself be the easiest? Why was it the hardest? It was a question Janet wished to answer over a bottle of vodka.

She had already gone three days without drinking. Her mind was sharper than it had been in years. She had assumed her drinking dulled it permanently, but it was an illusion from always being drunk. Her brain was undoubtedly damaged, but she could not perceive how. It wasn't damaged in the way she hoped, at least. One of her justifications for drinking was to selectively destroy the part of her brain that thinks uncomfortable thoughts. She hypothesized that her ancestors had evolved, in the presence of alcohol, an extra lobe in the brain to overcome their drunkenness. Without alcohol, this lobe was deleterious.

"It's the dumbest idea you ever had," chirped Finchoncho, who flew out of the plants behind Janet and onto the drooling face of President Sheethead.

"What are you," Janet started loudly before realizing she was shouting at no one, "doing here?" she finished in a whisper.

"I've always been here. I live in your brain, Janet."

"I mean why are you out of my brain and talking again? Can't I just talk to you in my head?"

"If you can't control your feelings, what makes you think you can control your fart hallucinations?"

Janet was stumped. For some reason she thought knowing the bird was a part of her imagination would make it disappear, but it was clearly untrue. She folded her arms and slouched. "Well, what wise words do you have for me this time? You want me to jump out a window or something?"

"No, Janet! No! I am just here to say 'hello'."

"Sure you are."

"And to tell you that you pity yourself far too much."

"Excuse me?"

"You heard me. You pity yourself as though you are still a child. It's pathetic! You're a grown woman and about to be the queen of

Earth. You are in the most comfortable seat in the galaxy eating the most delicious food ever invented. How can you possibly feel bad for yourself at a time like this? You think talking to a fart is crazy? No, Janet! Self-pity. This is the most insane thing you do."

"That's not a very nice thing to say to someone."

"Do you feel bad for yourself for hearing the truth from your own mind? This is craziness."

"So, I should just be happy about everything? Eat some cripnock and enjoy the Alien takeover?"

"Yes! Be happy! The Aliens have come. The Aliens have conquered. The Aliens have given us cripnock. Be happy, little human."

Janet sighed. There wasn't a reason for her to be upset. An alien did just take control of her country, but who's to say it was a bad thing? It was a thing that she associates with badness, but the moment-to-moment reality was quite good. Especially the moments when she was eating cripnock. Why was it so difficult to accept that she had been feeling sorry for herself unnecessarily? Yes, she had a very unusual childhood marked by loss and loneliness and times of true sorrow, but how much of her life was really that bad? How much of her life was miserable because she was imagining the sad things that happened in the past? Most of her life was just sitting or standing or walking or laying down and thinking about stuff while she does. Maybe it was the design of humans to feel bad about what they have to motivate themselves to get something better. Then again, Janet never did anything to try to improve her life before the bird showed up. Maybe it was all an effort to try to convince anyone who may stray into her life that she was deserving and requiring of help. Maybe it was an effort to escape responsibility. It was a disgusting thought, and yet the truth in it made it impossible to dismiss. For a moment,

Janet felt sorry for herself for realizing she had spent so much time feeling sorry for herself.

"You're doing it again!" sang the bird.

"I know I am, but I don't know how to stop!"

"It's simple, Janet. Just open your eyes and look around. See what the world is really like. The trees, the bees, and the air you sneeze! Where did they all come from? No one knows, but it is here for you. You can try to live in a world in your head, but you cannot imagine a single flea in its entirety! Recognize the grandness of reality and be grateful!"

"It's that simple? Just ditch my brain and eat cripnock?"

"Yes, Janet!"

Janet opened her mouth but couldn't think of anything to say. She was talking to herself after all. It would be ridiculous to argue. Instead, she took the advice and looked around the room. Everywhere she looked was as detailed as could be. The bird was right that she could not imagine anything as complex as the real world, let alone something that functions perfectly while adhering to the principles of physics. How does a handful of rules of motion turn a bunch of dots into a drooling President Sheethead? He was disgusting, but also fascinating. Even his drool was unimaginably detailed.

Realizing that even looking at the drool of a gross old man was more pleasant than slipping into her self-loathing, Janet decided to focus on what was around her. "Computer? Could I have another bowl of cripnock? Or maybe something else you think I would like?"

"It would be my pleasure," the computer responded. The arm from the ceiling dropped down with a plate of something like Janet had never seen before. It was orange and a foot tall. It was fibrous and dense. It looked juicy, but it was dry to the touch. "This is florm. It is a meal reserved for the most special occasions."

"Thank you," Janet said. "How do I eat it?"

"Grab a manageable piece with your hands and put it in your mouth."

"Oh," Janet mumbled. She tore off a chunk from the top. The fibers were tough enough to hold the piece firmly together in her hands, but fragile enough to be effortlessly torn to a desirable chunk. Janet wondered how this was possible. Were the fibers perforated in such a way to fail most easily to the specific stresses of grabbing and tearing? Is that even possible?

"The next step is to put it in your mouth," the computer reminded Janet.

Janet blushed and put the chunk of florm in her mouth. As she bit down, the flavor exploded. It was the most savory bite of food she ever had. The flavor knocked her back into her seat. She moaned as she chewed. The world was indeed a beautiful place.

"Would you like to watch where we are going?" The computer asked.

"Yes, please," Janet said while tearing off another chunk of florm.

"We are passing over the city," The computer said. The screen turned on, showing the view from below the spaceship.

Smoke streamed up from dozens of spots around the city. The bombing had begun, but the florm in Janet's mouth overwhelmed her instinct to grieve. She watched as though it were just colors on a screen, which, in truth, it was. "Are you spraying the city with Charlando's slime?" She asked.

"Yes."

"Do you think that will stop the fighting?"

"It already has."

Janet looked closer at the screen. There was no way to tell if that were true by the images it showed, but she believed it was so. This was not how she would have imagined the war to end, but she didn't know how the war started nor how anything worked on such a grand scale. How could she imagine how things should be if she didn't understand how anything worked? How could she tell what was good?

"Florm is good," Finchoncho chirped.

Yes, florm is good. Janet took another bite and continued watching the display. They left the city and flew over expansive fields of grains and vegetables. How much of those crops had she eaten without appreciation for how it came to exist?

The farms dwindled into open grassland. The wind rippled across it, exposing infinite shades of beige. The plains were much bigger than her little city, but they eventually ended. A line of mountains sprung suddenly towards her and dropped away just as abruptly. In its wake, a short stretch of bright green hills petered into a sparkling sea. If the grassland was big, the sea was beyond measure.

Janet stared and chewed chunk after chunk. Focusing on the world around her had indeed calmed her nerves, but her mind remained revved and ready to carry her back to misery. She tried holding on to the room around her, but the monotonous blue waters had little for her focus to grab onto. She tore the last piece of florm in half and stuffed both pieces in her mouth greedily. She needed more if she wanted to keep her calmness. Was florm any better than vodka in this regard? Janet felt herself slipping.

"How much farther do we have?" she asked the computer desperately.

"Twelve minutes."

"That's a relief. How long has it been since we flew over the city?"

"Seven minutes."

"That was only seven minutes!"

President Sheethead stirred in his slumber. She had only been able to go seven minutes without thinking about how hard her life was, and that was with a cubic foot of florm to eat. There were more than two-hundred seven-minute stretches in a day, and thousands of days left in her life. It was too much to handle.

"Don't worry about tomorrow," Finchoncho chirped. "There is nothing you can do outside of the present."

"I can't do this anymore. Why is this so hard?"

"How did you feel this morning?"

"This morning? I don't know. I was working all morning. I didn't feel anything."

"And what about yesterday? You got through yesterday easily enough."

"Yesterday was insane! I went to the biggest party I've ever seen. I got arrested and then broken out of jail. A war started. An alien professed his love for me and then sacrificed himself to save me. If that's what it takes for me to get through a day without drinking, I can't make it any longer."

"Did you throw the party? Did you start the war?"

"Of course not."

"Then why feel pressure to do it again? Trust the universe!"

"Why would I trust the universe? Those types of things don't happen every day you know. Years went by and nothing happened. This week was an anomaly. Why would a few days outweigh twenty-two years of experience?"

"The universe has never been less interesting. You have only now decided to engage with it. Keep moving and the universe will do the rest."

"I don't want to feel anything anymore. What will the universe have me do about that?"

"Eat more cripnock. Cripnock is good."

"I can't eat cripnock every moment of my life, Finchoncho!" Janet grabbed her hair and curled into a ball. All her muscles tensed, and her mind boiled in searing discontent.

Finchooncho hopped off President Sheethead's face and onto Janet's. "Eat cripnock. Eat cripnock," he said while pecking at Janet's forehead.

"Can I have more cripnock?" Janet blurted out desperately.

"Of course," the computer responded before swiftly dropping Janet a heaping bowl. Janet stuffed her face with a handful. It took another two bites for her muscles to unclench.

"Cripnock is good," the bird repeated while gently pecking her forehead.

"Is this how my life will be from now on? Just sitting and eating and feeling like death?"

"No," Finchoncho said. "You're an alcoholic. People feel bad after a single night of drinking. You were drunk for six years. It will take days and weeks to recover from that. For now, stay out of your head." He went back to poking Janet's forehead and chanting 'cripnock is good'.

This went on for the next eight minutes. Janet nearly cleared her bowl of cripnock while watching the ocean keep going and going. It started turning a lighter shade of blue. An island appeared and then vanished. They were getting closer. She saw white sand beneath the water, then waves crashing, and then a sprawling coastal city bustling below her. It was beautiful. They weaved through towering skyscrapers huddled by the beach reflecting the sparkling ocean in their windows. They whirled above sprawling neighborhoods flowing into the tree-covered hills behind the city. The spaceship ascended the highest hill with the largest houses and approached the largest of them all at the top of the hill. The spaceship shook as it landed.

President Sheethead jolted awake. "Where are we?" Sheethead asked. "You and I didn't..."

"We are at the palace of the Supreme Leader of Chumpkwee," the computer responded. "Please meet Charlando by the exit."

The president shot up at once and wiped the drool from his chin. "Yes, mam," he said before bolting out of the room, combing his hair over with his hands and straightening his tie as he went.

"Are you coming, Janet?" the computer asked.

Finchoncho nodded and bounced up and down on Janet's forehead. "I suppose so," she said. Janet followed the president to the exit. Charlando was waiting at the door. His smiling face was covered in slop. He too must have been eating for the entire ride. Maybe that was something they could do together.

The door opened to the outside. A wall of warm, humid air met them as they walked through and down the steps to a brick courtyard artfully laid around small fruit trees and fountains. Tropical birds and insects chirped and buzzed from the jungle surrounding the palace. Finchoncho flew off Janet's head towards them.

A family emerged from the creamy white palace dressed in bright, flowing clothing. The father, a fat bearded man, held his three curious children back as they approached. His wife walked elegantly beside him.

"Welcome to Chumpkwee," the fat man proclaimed when they got close enough. "It is an honor to treat with you. Please, my little green friend, allow me to gift you with whatever your heart desires!"

"Oh, I don't need anything," Charlando said. "Thank you."

"Yes you do," the computer objected. "Supreme Leader Plumpy, this is Charlando. He is the ruler of the now unified lands of Charlandia. His domain consists of all the former kingdoms of Chumpkwee and Goopland. You will give a joint press conference with Former President Sheethead in which you both declare fealty to

Charlando." Everyone but Charlando looked deeply confused by this development. Interestingly, Charlando probably also had the least understanding of what was happening.

"Is this true?" Plumpy asked. "Do you want the entire kingdom of Chumpkwee?"

"What should I say, Mother?" Charlando asked the spaceship.

"Yes," it replied.

"Then yes, I do want that."

"Very well," Plumpy said solemnly. "I will call for a press release."

"There is no need," the computer said. "I will broadcast your resignations myself."

Both Plumpy and Sheethead were completely emasculated. They offered no resistance as they shuffled to a spot in front of a fountain where the computer told them to go. Charlando joined them. Janet stood in the background with Plumpy's wife and kids.

The two leaders shook hands and proclaimed the ends of their respective countries. Charlando looked dumber than Janet had ever seen. This was the hero that ended the great war. It didn't matter that he was an idiot. Idiots are easily manipulated, and the computer has complete control of him. It was the computer who was in charge. Charlando was just the image on the screen for people to celebrate. Who then was Janet?

Janet wondered what Plumpy's wife did all day. She looked petrified. Was she also unaffected by the pheromones? There were bound to be more than just her and Bob who were immune. Considering the small sample size of people she knew to interact with Charlando, there was no knowing the actual rate of success of the pheromone. Considering two were immune within the small sample Janet saw, there would likely be millions amongst the general population. Time would tell.

It dawned on Janet that there would be a lot of confused people in the new land of Charlandia. Given Charlando's complete and utter stupidity, it would be up to her and the computer to sort things out. Did the computer already have a plan for all the unpossessed people? Would a new war break out between the Charlando supporters and the people who have no idea what was going on? Was it Janet's responsibility to protect those unaffected humans from whatever the computer had planned?

Janet slipped into her mind again, but not down her usual spiral. She emerged quickly and with a different outlook on her life. Not only did she not feel sorry for herself, she felt like she owed something to the world. It was a good feeling. Empowering.

Something else came into her mind. The computer had told her that Charlando loves her the same way his pheromones made others love him. If that were true, then she was the one with all the power. Charlando trusted the computer because it took care of him for so long, but he showed earlier that he would sooner sacrifice himself for Janet than take care of himself. This ceremony was not crowning Charlando, it was crowning her. Charlando would be a puppet to her and a hero to everyone else.

Janet put a hand on Plumpy's wife's arm and told her everything would be alright. She then stepped forward next to Charlando. His slop-covered face beamed at the sight of her. Janet smiled back. "I want to live in a palace just like this one," she said.

"I'm sure Mother can find you one," Charlando offered.

"I think you're old enough to not be so reliant on your mother," Janet replied. "I will look after you now."

Charlando looked longingly at his spaceship before turning back to Janet and smiling as wide as anyone had ever smiled. "I have dreamed my whole life for this moment," he said. "I will do whatever you want, my love."

The End...

Acknowledgements

Some of you may be wondering where I found the photographs of Charlando and Janet shown on the cover and title page of this book. As shocking as it may seem, those are not in fact photographs but drawings by the most talented artist in the world, Yvette Gilbert.

I found Yvette in a pub in a small town in Northern Ireland. She drank alone, and by the looks of things, she had no other options. There was something odd about her.

Curiosity made me take a closer look. I'm so fortunate I did. It was her immense talent bulging out of her that made her so strange to look at. Even more striking, was the odd way she spoke. "Beep, bop, boop," she said. "Beep, beep, boop, bop." The poor girl was so talented that she could only speak in 'beeps', 'boops' and 'bops'.

I had to do something. I had seen this before in a young boy from Paraguay. If she didn't start creating something soon, she would explode from the building pressure of her untapped genius. Who knows how many casualties there would have been?

I grabbed a pen from behind the bar and a napkin from the lap of the passed-out patron two stools down. "Do you know who Charlando is?" I asked, clear and direct.

"Bop boop," she repeated and nodded her head once.

Of course she does, I thought. Who doesn't know about Charlando?

"Draw Charlando," I told her. "And Janet, too." I didn't bother asking if she knew about Janet. I don't care how far gone a person is, they will know about Janet.

She began to draw. It was so beautiful I wept. All that untapped talent flowed through her hand and onto the page. As she did the lumps on her face and arms receded. Her rasping breath turned to calm. Her cloudy eyes turned clear and twinkly.

She pushed the napkin back to me. "Thank you," she said with relief. She then bounced off her stool and danced a joyful jig. She danced that joyful jig right on out of the pub, and down a long winding road to somewhere I'll never know.

Thank you, Yvette, wherever you are.

Made in the USA
Monee, IL
15 October 2024

67249751R10135